SECOND CHANCES

A LATER IN LIFE LOVE STORY

DIANA XARISSA

✾ Created with Vellum

For my cozy readers who are coming along with me to Ramsey, New York.

Welcome to Ramsey, New York – a small town full of characters. Some are looking for love, some most definitely are not. Sooner or later, everyone finds his or her happily ever after.

CHAPTER 1

"*N*ot long now," Karen Henderson-Archer said with a bright smile as she handed an envelope to Camille Quinn.

"The kids still have a few weeks of summer vacation yet," Camille countered. "I don't know about your two, but mine are doing everything they can to slow down time."

Karen laughed. "We're off on our big family vacation starting tomorrow. That's why I brought all of the paperwork in today. I hope that's everything you need."

Camille opened the envelope and looked through the contents. "Physical exam results for both children, updated emergency contact information, and an application for a parking permit for Donald, Junior. I think that's all that we need, at this point, anyway."

"No doubt on the first day of school you'll send home a dozen other things that I'll need to complete," Karen said with a shrug. "It happens every year, no matter how organized I try to be."

As your staff does all of your organizing for you, ·I'm not impressed, Camille thought. "Let me get a parking permit for Donald, then," she said, getting to her feet.

"His father and I bought him a small SUV. We wanted something with four-wheel drive for the winter months."

"So do I," Camille muttered as she pulled down the box with the parking permits inside. She loved her job at Ramsey High School, thoroughly enjoying working with the students, the teachers, and the administration. The benefits were generous, but her salary was not. She just about made ends meet, but there wasn't room in the budget for a better car, not in the foreseeable future, anyway.

She filled out the required information on the tag and handed it to Karen. "Donald needs to hang this from his rearview mirror whenever he parks in the school lot," she told Karen. "If the tag isn't clearly visible, the car may get towed."

Karen made a face. "We've been friends forever, so you can be honest with me. Does the school ever actually have any cars towed?"

We've known each other since kindergarten, but I've never considered us friends, Camille thought. "It has been known to happen," she replied. "Just tell Donald to use the tag."

"The color will clash with his all black leather interior," Karen complained as she tucked the bright green tag into her handbag.

Camille raised an eyebrow. That was an excuse she'd not heard before, anyway.

"And now I must dash," Karen said. "I'm so happy you were here today to deal with all of this. I was worried the school might be closed for the summer months."

"Technically, we are closed, but I'm putting in some extra hours helping some of the teachers get ready for a few of the new classes available this year." *And making some extra money that's always needed,* she added to herself.

"Junior said something about some new classes, but he wasn't interested in any of them. He wants to be a doctor, of course, following in his father's footsteps, you understand. He'll be taking AP science and math classes to get ready for college and then medical school."

Camille nodded. "I can't believe our children are going to be juniors."

"I remember my junior year as if it were yesterday," Karen told her. "After all of the hours that we spent in these corridors while we were students, I'm amazed you wanted to come back here to work."

"I love my job."

"And I love not having to work at all," Karen laughed. "Of course, I hate the long hours that poor Donald puts in at the hospital and in his practice, but I can't complain about all of the lovely money that his hard work provides."

Camille forced herself to smile. "I didn't work when the children were small, and I found that I missed it."

"And then your husband ran off with another woman and you had no choice but to go back to work."

While that wasn't exactly what had happened, Camille didn't bother to argue. "And I was very fortunate to find the job here at the high school. The kids and I get the same vacation days, and I'm usually off all summer, as well."

"Except you're working today."

"As I said, I came in to help out a few teachers who are putting together new classes. They have a lot to do before the first day of school."

"So do I," Karen said, glancing at her gold watch. "As I said, we leave in the morning for two weeks of sun and fun. Well, I do anyway. Karly is doing a cheer camp that doesn't finish until Friday, so she'll fly down to join me once that's done. Junior is doing some sort of community service project, so he won't be joining me until Sunday. And, of course, Donald forgot to write the dates on his calendar so he has a full schedule of surgeries and whatnot for the entire two weeks. I'm hoping he might make it down for a weekend, anyway."

"At least you'll have fun," Camille suggested.

"Oh, I will. I love lying on the beach and drinking margaritas all day. It's such a nice break from everything here. Have you had a wonderful summer vacation trip somewhere yet?"

"Not this summer. Brandon has been working a great deal and they've both been training, as well. Besides that, I've been teaching Brandon to drive."

"Training?" Karen frowned. "Oh, that's right, they do karate or judo or something similar, don't they?"

"They do Tae Kwon Do. Brandon is a second degree black belt and Molly will be earning her black belt in December."

"How nice," Karen said breezily. "I was so grateful to Donald's driver. He taught Junior how to drive. I still haven't been in a car with Junior driving and I don't really intend to be."

The phone on the desk buzzed and Camille couldn't answer it fast enough. She waved at Karen as she spoke into the receiver, hoping that the other woman would take the hint and leave while she was on the phone.

"Ramsey High School, this is Camille. How can I help you?"

"It's Jana Bailey. I was just wondering when schedules would be available."

"They'll be sent electronically to all students on Friday," Camille replied. "We'll also be putting paper copies in the mail on Friday, so you should have those by Monday."

"Excellent. Shawn is very excited to see what classes he has this year."

"That's good to hear. I don't think my two are excited exactly."

Jana laughed. "Excited might be the wrong word, but he is hoping to get a few more interesting classes now that he's in high school."

"We do have a wide range of interesting classes. I hope he gets what he wants."

"Thank you."

Camille put the phone down and looked back up at Karen. "Was there anything else?" she asked.

Karen tossed her head. "I simply didn't want to be rude and walk away while you were on the phone," she said. "It was lovely to see you again, though. We should have a class reunion, just for the people who've stayed in Ramsey. There are quite a few of us, really."

"It was nice to see you, too," Camille replied flatly.

Karen grabbed her huge designer handbag off the desk and headed for the door. On the threshold, she turned back. "Oh, I nearly forgot. I suppose you've already heard, though."

Camille froze, certain of what was coming next. "Heard?" she echoed.

"Max is back in town. I was sure you'd have heard."

"Max?"

Karen laughed. "Now I know you're teasing. Max, as in Maxwell Steward. I'm sure you remember him. He was tall, dark, and handsome back in the day."

Camille felt a rush of color flood her cheeks. "I remember him," she admitted.

"You two were inseparable in high school," Karen remembered. "Of course, he was two years ahead of us, but you started dating him when you were a freshman, didn't you?"

"I was only fourteen. It wasn't anything serious," Camille replied, blinking hard and trying to suppress both memories and the flood of emotions that talking about Max always caused.

"But you were together all through high school and college, weren't you?" Karen demanded.

"We both stayed in Ramsey for college but we broke up when he graduated."

"Of course, because he wanted to go to New York and find fame and fortune."

Camille nodded, swallowing hard to push down the lump in her throat. Max had left for New York City something like thirty years earlier, but sometimes she felt as if the pain of his going was still fresh.

"He certainly found fortune," Karen continued. "Did you see the car he's driving around town in? It's one of those fancy sports cars with the doors that open up vertically. Donald is jealous, but we have two kids to put through college. I don't think Max ever married."

"I have no idea," Camille said, trying to sound unconcerned. She'd done her best to avoid hearing anything about the man for the last thirty years. In her imagination, he'd had nothing but short-term, unhappy relationships. She didn't want to know differently.

"Once I'm back from my vacation, I should have you and Max over for dinner," Karen said thoughtfully. "I'm sure you'd love to see him again, wouldn't you?"

"Not really," Camille lied. "I can't imagine we have anything in common anymore."

"No, I suppose you don't," Karen agreed. She shrugged and then turned and walked out of the room, leaving Camille frowning at her disappearing back.

She was still frowning when her closest friend, Terri Briggs, walked into the office a few minutes later.

"What's wrong?" Terri asked as a greeting.

"What makes you think something is wrong?" Camille countered.

"You look either mad at the world or as if you're going to cry, I'm not certain which."

Camille forced herself to chuckle. "I'm fine," she said dully.

"Of course you are, but what's wrong?"

"Karen Henderson-Archer was here," Camille explained. "She needed a parking permit for Donald, Junior's shiny new car."

"And that made you feel bad because you can't afford to buy Brandon a new car?"

"Partly. She also made sure to mention that Max is back in town."

"Ouch," Terri made a face. The two friends had shared their life stories with one another, so Terri understood exactly how much Max had meant to Camille and how upset she was about his return. "That should get easier once you've actually seen him again for yourself," she suggested.

"I hope I never see him. He's probably just in town to show off his fancy car and his expensive watch. No doubt he'll get bored with Ramsey quickly enough and head right back to the big city where he belongs."

"Someone told me he's been looking around the Alexander house."

"Of course he is," Camille said sharply. "Because buying the Alexander house was always my dream and Max is never happier than when he's destroying my dreams. He probably only came back here so that he can buy the house, just to keep me from ever having a chance to do so."

Terri raised an eyebrow. "Do you really think he'd do that?"

Camille took a deep breath and then wiped away a stray

tear. "No, not really," she admitted. "He probably doesn't even remember me telling him that I'd always wanted to buy the Alexander house. I could just see a bit of the mansion from my childhood bedroom window. There were nearly always lights on inside the house and it looked like a fairytale castle or something. I've never actually been inside, though. I've heard it's in terrible condition."

"That's what I've heard as well. I thought about looking at it when I was house hunting, but whatever condition it's in, it was still way above my budget."

"Yeah, it's way above mine, too," Camille admitted. "I can barely afford my house. Max is welcome to the Alexander house, I suppose."

"Are you okay? I mean, for money? I can help out a little bit if you…" Terri trailed off as Camille held up a hand.

"I'm fine," she said firmly. "Money is always going to be tight, especially since Jason never sends what he's supposed to send for the children, but we're surviving. As long as I don't have any unexpected expenses, we'll be just fine, even if we can't afford to buy a mansion."

"Karen lives in a mansion and I don't think she's very happy," Terri pointed out.

"I wouldn't be happy either, if I were married to Donald," Camille laughed.

She didn't feel as much like laughing when she got out of work a few hours later. It was already five o'clock and she still needed to stop at the grocery store on her way home. Then she had to make dinner, feed herself and the children, and then get the kids to Tae Kwon Do. Molly had class at seven and Camille was supposed to take Brandon driving while Molly was in class. Then Brandon was supposed to be taking the eight o'clock class. Now she was tired and all she wanted to do was soak in a hot bath with a glass of wine and a good book.

"We don't have any wine or any new books in the house," she reminded herself as she slid behind the wheel of her small car.

It had been the perfect car for her when they'd bought it, ten years earlier. She'd needed something to get the kids from school to their activities and to run errands in, nothing more. Jason had had a large SUV that they'd used for family excursions and large shopping trips. Five years later, however, Jason had decided he'd had enough of family life in a small town, leaving her on her own with the children. Now, the car was showing its age, but there wasn't any money in the budget to replace it.

She ran through the grocery store as quickly as she could, grabbing essentials. Mentally planning what she was going to cook for dinner, she drove home on autopilot, pulling the car onto the driveway without really noticing the journey. As she climbed out of the car, she paused, as she always did, and smiled at the house. It had been her home for nearly all of her life. Her parents had bought the house when she'd been a baby and she'd grown up in one of the small bedrooms on the second floor.

When she and Jason had first been married, they'd rented an apartment near the college, but they'd moved in with Camille's parents when she'd been pregnant with Brandon. It was an arrangement that had suited everyone, especially after Camille's father had passed away. When Camille's mother died, she left the house to Camille and in spite of her talk about the Alexander mansion, Camille couldn't imagine living anywhere else.

"I made cupcakes," Molly told Camille as she walked into the house.

"Cupcakes?" Camille repeated, feeling confused.

"I thought it would be nice to have a treat after dinner,"

Molly explained. "I baked cupcakes and Brandon helped me wash the dishes and clean up the kitchen when I was done."

Camille carried the shopping bags into the kitchen as her daughter was talking. A quick glance around the room revealed that the children hadn't cleaned up everything, but Camille was grateful that they'd tried, at least.

"I thought I'd make spaghetti," Camille said.

"Yay," Molly cheered.

Half an hour later, the trio sat down to dinner with Molly's chocolate cupcakes for dessert.

"Mom?" Brandon asked as they ate. "Have you thought any more about getting a second car?"

Camille frowned. "I told you a second car was out of the question for now."

"I know, but I thought maybe you'd changed your mind," Brandon said with a sigh.

"I'll do my best to let you drive my car, er, rather, our car, once you have your license, but adding you to the insurance is going to cost a fair bit, or so I'm told. I can't imagine what insuring a second car would cost, even if I could afford to buy one," Camille told him.

"I was at one of the used car lots today and they had cars for as little as a thousand dollars," Brandon replied.

"I wouldn't let you drive around in a car that only cost a thousand dollars. I want you in something safe and road worthy."

"I'm not certain your car qualifies, then," Brandon muttered.

Camille flushed. "It's all we have," she sighed. *And if your father would pay what he's supposed to pay, I might be able to replace it.* She never said anything to the children about the money Jason was meant to be sending. That was between her and him and not their concern. He was only sporadically in touch with the children, ringing once every few months from wherever he happened to be staying at the time.

After dinner, the children changed into their uniforms and the trio headed out. Camille parked at the Tae Kwon Do school and then walked Molly inside. While she was doing that, Brandon moved the seat and the mirrors so that he could drive.

"Everything set?" she checked as she settled into the passenger seat.

"Yep. I've put the seat back as far as it will go, but I still feel cramped."

Camille laughed. "What can I tell you? You're too tall."

Brandon took after his father and at six feet tall, he seemed to tower over his mother who was six inches shorter. Molly seemed to be doing her best to catch her brother, as well.

Brandon started the car and then very carefully pulled out of the parking lot.

"Turn right at the traffic light," Camille told him. "This is a very tight corner, so make sure you take the turn carefully even if the light is green."

"Yes, mother," Brandon muttered. He slowed down and then turned the wheel to the right.

"Slow down more," Camille said as she spotted the approaching car. "And turn more tightly."

"I don't want to hit the curb," Brandon objected as he went just a bit too widely around the corner.

Camille winced as she heard the sound of the impact and then breaking glass. They hadn't been going very fast, but clearly some damage had been done.

"Pull the car into the parking lot here," she told Brandon, hoping against hope that the damage would all be to her car and inexpensive to repair.

The car that Brandon had hit spun around and followed them into the lot.

"Wow, I've never seen a car with scissor doors in real life," Brandon said as the driver of the other car opened his door.

Camille looked over at it and a string of curse words sprang to her lips. She swallowed hard, and then banged her head back against the headrest. This was just about the worst possible occasion for her to see Maxwell Steward again.

CHAPTER 2

"*O*ut you get," she told Brandon. "Time to learn how to deal with an accident."

Brandon made a face. "Can't you just…" he began.

Camille shook her head and then unfastened her seatbelt and slowly opened her door. Her heart sank when she saw the damage to the expensive sports car.

"It looks as if your bumper was in just the wrong place," a voice said from behind her.

Camille turned around and tried to smile at the man standing there. He looked around forty, and he was wearing a suit that Camille was fairly certain was worth more than her car.

"Sorry," Brandon muttered. "I guess I took out your headlight."

The other man nodded. "I'm Seth Pierce, Maxwell Steward's assistant." He gestured toward Maxwell who was standing behind his car, talking on his cell phone. "Max asked me to get all of your information while he deals with rearranging an appointment."

"I'm really sorry," Brandon said, his face bright red.

Seth shrugged. "Accidents happen. It's a tight corner. I'm going to guess you haven't been driving for long."

"I'm still learning," Brandon admitted.

"I'll need your license and insurance information," Seth told him.

"Maybe we don't need to involve the insurance companies," Camille said tentatively. "It's just a headlight, after all. Maybe I can simply pay for a replacement."

"I'd still like to have your information, just in case," Seth replied.

Camille flushed. "Of course. I'm not trying to cheat anyone or anything, but my car insurance is going to skyrocket when I add Brandon to the policy. Adding an accident as well will probably make it completely unaffordable."

"You might be surprised how much a headlight for this car costs," Seth warned her.

Sighing deeply, Camille walked back over to the car and got out the registration and insurance cards from the glove compartment. Seth took pictures of Brandon's permit and the cards and then handed them all back to Camille.

"I'll give you my card," he said, pulling a silver card case out of his pocket. "I'd rather you didn't bother Mr. Steward with any of this."

Camille had been doing her best not to look at Max, but now she glanced over at him and immediately regretted it as their eyes met. She felt herself blushing brightly, but Max didn't seem to recognize her. He nodded curtly and then turned around and continued his phone conversation.

"Call me when you have an estimate on what the repairs will cost," Camille said, struggling to retain her composure. "I'll start hunting behind the sofa cushions for spare change."

Seth laughed. "Good luck with that. I'll be in touch, probably early tomorrow."

"If no one answers, you can leave a message on the machine," Camille told him.

He nodded and then turned and walked over to Max. Camille rushed back to her own car and climbed back into the passenger seat. Brandon followed more slowly.

"Maybe you should just drive," he said as he slid behind the wheel.

Camille watched as Max and Seth got back into Max's car. As Max roared away, she turned and smiled at Brandon.

"It's a tight corner and you're still learning. Accidents happen. I was supervising you, so it's as much my fault as it is yours."

Brandon shook his head. "You told me to slow down and turn more tightly. I should have listened."

"And we can sit here all night debating what you should have done differently, or we can get some driving practice in before time for your class. We can't change the past, so we may as well focus on the future."

Brandon didn't look as if he agreed, but after a moment he fastened his seatbelt and started the car. Camille was silent as he very carefully pulled out of the parking lot and slowly began to drive down the road.

"How much do you think it will cost to get that fancy car fixed?" Brandon asked as they went.

"I've no idea. From what I could see, the headlight was broken, but there wasn't any other damage. Our car doesn't seem to have a scratch on it."

"I've been working all summer. I can pay for it."

"You've been working all summer to earn money for college, not car repairs."

"Yeah, but you've been working all summer, too, and I'm pretty sure none of that money was intended for car repairs, either," Brandon countered.

Camille flushed. "I've told you before that I don't want you worrying about money."

"I'm sixteen and I'm reasonably bright. I know money is tight, and I know that Dad doesn't help out, even though he should."

"We're doing okay. I have an emergency fund to cover things like unexpected car repairs. Turn left at the stop sign." Camille was determined to change the subject before Brandon asked her any more questions about money.

The rest of the drive was uneventful and they were back at the Tae Kwon Do school with time to spare.

"I think I might skip class tonight," Brandon said as he parked the car. "I'm not really feeling up to it."

"You should go," Camille told him. "Kicking someone always makes you feel better."

Brandon laughed. "I know you're right, but I feel terrible about the accident."

"Let me worry about the accident. I'm the mother. It's my job to do all of the worrying about adult stuff. You have enough of your own things to worry about, like school, and college, and that cute girl in your math class."

"There aren't any cute girls in my math class."

"No?"

"Maybe one or two, but I don't like any of them."

Camille laughed. "That's fine with me. You can date after college. That's soon enough."

"I didn't say I didn't like any girls, just not the ones in math."

Brandon was out of the car before Camille could respond. She followed more slowly, wondering if she needed to have another talk with him about girls.

Molly was standing near the door when Camille walked into the building.

"Ready for home?" Camille asked her.

"Totally. Master Caldwell made us work extra hard tonight. He said we're all getting lazy because it's summer vacation."

"He's probably right."

Molly frowned and then laughed. "He is right, actually, but I'm only lazy at home. I've been working really hard here."

"That's because you're testing for black belt in December. You need to work extra hard."

"Yes, mother, I know," Molly sighed.

Camille laughed before she and Molly walked back to the car. Before she climbed inside, Molly looked hard at the bumper.

"I don't see any marks," she said.

"How did you already hear about the accident?" Camille demanded.

"Karly texted me that Brandon hit Max Steward's million dollar sports car. She said she'd heard that he'd caused like half a million dollars in damage. I was expecting our car to be wrecked, really."

Camille shook her head. "The gossip network in this town is incredible. Brandon barely tapped Max's car. A headlight was broken, but that was all the damage. The car isn't worth a million dollars, either." *I hope*, she added to herself.

Molly shrugged. "Karly said that her mom told her that you and Max had history. What does that mean?"

"Get in the car," Camille suggested. "We can talk at home." There were too many people getting in and out of cars in the parking lot for Camille to want to have a conversation about Max there. She was silent on the drive back to their house, not certain how much she wanted to tell Molly about her past with Max.

When they got home, Camille made hot chocolate for

both of them. She gave Molly a few chocolate chip cookies to go with her drink.

"So tell me about Max," Molly said around a mouthful of cookie.

"Since when are you such good friends with Karly Archer?"

Molly shrugged. "We aren't friends. I'm not even sure how she got my number. Everyone in the whole town is talking about Max Steward, though. I think she only texted me because she wanted to hear what he'd said to Brandon after Brandon smashed into his really, really expensive car."

"Brandon didn't smash into anything. It was a fender bender, if that. We aren't even involving the insurance companies." *I hope*, Camille added silently.

"But you did get to speak to Max Steward, anyway," Molly said excitedly.

"We didn't, actually. His assistant, Seth something-or-other, spoke with us."

Molly made a face. "That isn't going to make for such an exciting story."

"Sorry about that."

"But you did know Max when he lived here before, didn't you?" Molly demanded.

Camille nodded. "I did know him years ago, yes."

"Karly said that her mother said that you and Max were a couple."

Thanks, Karen, Camille thought. "We dated when I was in high school," she said, still not certain how much she wanted to share with her daughter. Molly was twelve, old enough to hear some of the story, anyway, she decided.

"Did you date for long?"

"We dated for six years, until Max finished college."

"Six years? That's a long time," Molly said. "What happened when Max graduated?"

Camille took a sip of her drink and then sighed. "He dumped me," she said simply, sternly ordering herself not to cry.

Molly frowned. "Why would he do that? He must be stupid."

Camille chuckled. "He wanted to go to New York City and make himself a fortune. I still had two years of college to finish and he didn't want to wait. I refused to drop out of school for him and he refused to wait for me."

"That was brave of you."

"Was it?" Camille asked. She hadn't really thought about it that way at the time. Not long before his graduation, Max had casually mentioned that he was planning to leave Ramsey. She'd been shocked and upset by the news. He'd suggested that she might consider coming with him, but she was determined to finish her degree. As a first generation college student whose parents were sacrificing a lot to pay her tuition, she hadn't felt as if she had much choice. When she'd told Max she wasn't coming with him, he'd seemed more relieved than anything else.

"I think so," Molly said firmly. "Anyway, then you met Dad and fell in love with him."

"It wasn't quite like that," Camille said with a laugh. "I already knew your father. He'd been at school with me, the same as Max. They were friends, actually."

"Really? I didn't know that Dad knew Max Steward."

"They were friends in high school, but then your father went away to college. We reconnected at my ten-year high school reunion, actually."

"Max didn't come?"

"It wasn't his reunion. Besides, as far as I know, this is the first time Max has been back in Ramsey since he left within days of his college graduation," Camille told her. "He didn't even come back when his father died, although he did fly his mother to the Bahamas for a lengthy vacation after the funeral."

"So why is he back now?"

"I've no idea."

"What did he say when you saw him tonight?"

"I didn't speak to him. We talked to his assistant. Max was on the other side of the parking lot, talking on his cell phone the entire time."

Molly frowned. "You're going to have to try harder, Mom."

"Try harder at what?"

"Getting back together with Max, of course. He's a billionaire now. How amazing is that?"

"It's pretty amazing, even if it isn't true," Camille said dryly. "He's quite wealthy, but I don't think he's a billionaire."

"Billionaire, millionaire, whatever, he's rich, really rich, and you used to be in love with him, right? You just have to find a way to meet up with him again and then fall back in love. He'll fall in love with you easily enough. You're amazing. Then you can have a big, expensive wedding and we'll all live happily ever after."

Camille wasn't sure if she wanted to laugh or cry. "Dearest daughter, I'm afraid life doesn't work that way. Yes, I was in love with Max once, but that was more than thirty years ago. We aren't the same people we were then. There's a very good chance we wouldn't even like one another if we did get a chance to meet again."

"Six years, Mom. You grew up together. That has to count for something."

"Look him up online," Camille suggested. "You'll find tons of photos of him coming out of nightclubs with gorgeous blonde supermodels on his arm. I'm too old to go clubbing and I'm certainly not a supermodel."

Molly looked at her critically. "You aren't in bad shape," she said after a moment. "How tall are you?"

"Five feet, seven, if I stand very straight."

"Supermodels tend to be too thin, anyway. You're a healthy weight for your height. You should probably do something with your hair, though."

Camille ran her fingers through her shoulder-length brown bob. It was easy to take care of and if she didn't look too closely, she barely noticed the grey hairs that were slowly taking over her head. "My hair is fine," she snapped.

"You would look good blonde."

"I've been blonde. It needs too much upkeep," Camille told her. She'd been blonde throughout most of her marriage, actually, and she wasn't interested in going there again.

"Maybe just a few highlights, then?" Molly suggested.

"Maybe I'll stay just the way I am," Camille replied. *And stay well away from Maxwell Steward, as well*, she added to herself.

"But if you and Max got back together, think how wonderful things would be for me and Brandon."

Camille drew a sharp breath. "I doubt very much that Max is interested in being a step-father. Not that it matters, as I'm certain he isn't interested in dating a woman in her early fifties. I'm not his type, not anymore."

Molly sighed. "Maybe, just for tonight, I'll pretend you and Max are getting back together. It would be like winning the lottery and you let me imagine how wonderful that would be."

"Except I never buy tickets for the lottery."

"I know, but I still dream," Molly told her. "Imagine having millions of dollars in the bank. We could have a proper vacation somewhere wonderful and Brandon and I could both go to college, as well."

"You and Brandon can both go to college. You and Brandon are both going to college. I've told you before not to worry about that."

Molly shrugged. "If you say so."

"I do say so and I'm the mother so you have to listen to me," Camille said firmly. "You can dream all you like about lottery wins, but no dreaming about me and Max getting back together. That's never going to happen. Regardless of how he feels about me, after the way he treated me, I would never be able to trust him again."

Sighing deeply, Molly finished her hot chocolate and put her mug in the dishwasher. "I'm going to go and read a book," she told her mom. "You're going to get Brandon soon, right?"

"I need to go now, actually," Camille said after glancing at the clock. "I'll be back soon. No wild parties while I'm gone."

"There go my plans for the next ten minutes," Molly said with a huge, fake sigh.

Laughing, Camille headed back out to the car. A quick glance at the bumper confirmed that it hadn't suffered any damage in the accident. She just had to hope that getting Max's car repaired wasn't going to cost her a fortune.

Brandon was ready to go when she arrived.

"The whole town is talking about my accident," he complained as she drove them home.

"Something else will happen tomorrow that will be more exciting," she replied.

He shrugged. "I hope so."

A short while later, she tucked each of the children into bed for the night.

"I have to be at work at seven," Brandon reminded her.

"Yes, I know," she sighed. The Tae Kwon Do school had a summer camp program and Brandon loved being on the camp staff. It meant early starts for both him and Camille, though, at least a few mornings each week.

"Can I go to Katie's house tomorrow?" Molly asked as Camille straightened her bedding.

"I suppose so. What time?"

"She said I could come over when I got up and stay all day. We're going to swim."

"I'll call her mom in the morning."

"You don't have to call her mom. We've arranged everything."

"You know better than that."

Molly sighed. "You don't trust me to arrange things."

"I don't trust Katie to arrange things," Camille countered. "She doesn't have the best track record."

Molly giggled. "Okay, fair enough."

Katie had a bad habit of inviting Molly to visit every time they spoke without giving any thought to what else was happening in her life. Once, Molly had turned up for an afternoon in Katie's pool and found that the entire family, Katie included, had left for a week in Florida that morning.

An hour later, the dishwasher emptied and the house tidied, Camille crawled into bed. Thursday was going to be busy, but if she could get through it, she was going to be having dinner with Terri. A night out with her best friend was exactly what she needed at the moment, she decided as she snuggled under the covers.

CHAPTER 3

*C*amille dropped Brandon off at work and then went home and called Katie's mother. She was pleased to learn that Katie had actually already spoken to her and Molly was truly welcome to spend the day with her friend. With both children out for the morning, Camille ran errands and had a quick lunch before it was time to collect them both again.

"Behave tonight. Don't destroy anything," she told them as she headed for the door after she'd given them their dinner.

"There go my plans," Brandon sighed.

"I'll make sure he behaves," Molly assured her.

Camille laughed. "I'm not too worried. I won't be out for long."

"No rush. The longer you're out, the more time I get on the computer," Brandon replied.

Molly made a face. "I was going to go on the computer."

"We'll take turns," Brandon promised.

Camille decided not to get involved in their argument. Instead, she left, ready for some time with her friend.

"You look fabulous," she told Terri when she joined her at the corner table of their favorite restaurant.

"Just a little thing from the back of my closet," Terri said with a laugh. "I used to wear these sorts of things all the time, of course."

Terri was wearing a classic little black dress, her long blonde hair pulled up in a fancy sparkly clip. Camille knew that Terri's ex-husband had taken her to a lot of special events when they'd been married. He'd worked in public relations for a large company in New York City at the time. Camille had seen the inside of Terri's closet once and she'd been amazed at the number of gorgeous gowns her friend owned. There weren't many places or occasions for her to wear them in Ramsey, though.

As she slid into her chair, Camille glanced down at her own outfit. She was wearing a sundress, but she looked underdressed next to her glamorous friend. "I should have made more of an effort," she said apologetically.

"I'm overdressed," Terri shrugged. "It doesn't matter."

"So what's new?"

Terri laughed. "Since yesterday, not much. I understand your life in the past twenty-four hours has been a bit more exciting than mine, though."

"I'm not sure exciting is the word I would use."

"You crashed into Max Steward. Every single woman in Ramsey has been trying to get a chance to talk to him since he came home and you literally ran right into him."

"I wasn't driving."

"Is Brandon okay? Was he very upset?"

"He was upset, but I made him keep driving and I think he's mostly over it. He's worried about what it's going to cost to get the car fixed, though."

"Your car or Max's?"

"My car doesn't seem to have a scratch on it. Max's car has a broken headlight, though."

"I can't imagine a headlight will cost much."

"Except Max will probably want to take the car back to the city to get it fixed. I doubt any of the garages here work on cars like his, at least not often."

"You're probably right about that," Terri said, giving Camille's arm a sympathetic pat. "But tell me about Max. How did he look?"

"Distant," Camille said dryly.

"Distant?"

"As in, he stood on the opposite side of the car, talking on his cell phone, the entire time. His assistant, Seth Pierce, took all of our insurance information."

"He has an assistant? Of course he does. I'm surprised his assistant isn't a beautiful woman, actually."

Camille shrugged. "I'm sure, with his money, he could hire a dozen beautiful women if he wanted them. He may even have several assistants, but the one we met last night was a man in his forties."

"How did Max look, really?"

"Honestly? He looked gorgeous," Camille sighed. "He was really cute when he was younger, but now he's handsome. His dark brown hair had some grey through it, but it made him look distinguished, not old. His suit probably cost more than my house is worth, and it fit him perfectly. I'm certain he must work out, because no one could look that good at our age without some effort."

"He didn't talk to you?"

"Not at all. He barely glanced at me and I doubt very much he recognized me."

"Do you look very different from when you were younger?"

Camille shrugged. "I'm fifty-one. The last time he saw me,

I was nineteen. I think I probably look nothing like my old self."

"But you recognized him."

"His picture is in the paper every other day. I've had no choice but to watch him age."

"The local paper does like to brag about its former residents who do well. What did Jason say about the car accident?"

"I haven't spoken to Jason about it. I don't know if Brandon will mention it when he next talks to his father or not. They don't speak very often, though."

"Didn't you tell me that Jason and Max were friends in school?"

"They were, yes."

"I wonder if Jason knows that Max is back in town."

"I've no idea, and I can't see that it matters."

Terri laughed. "I'm sorry. I know you don't like talking about Jason."

"I don't like to think about him, let alone talk about him."

"He's a horrible person and you're better off without him," Terri told her firmly.

Camille nodded. "I just wish I'd realized that before I married him, except if I hadn't married him, I wouldn't have Brandon and Molly, and that would be worse. In spite of everything, I'm grateful to Jason for giving me Brandon and Molly."

"Now if he would just support them properly," Terri suggested.

"I'm doing okay. I've even managed to save some money. I'm hoping to take the kids on a trip next summer before Brandon starts his senior year."

"That would be nice for all of you."

"We haven't had a proper vacation since Jason left. We all need one."

"I suppose I can't complain about my ex, really, can I? He made me leave the big city and move to a small town in the middle of nowhere and then he left me, but I love Ramsey and I'm happier here than I've ever been. He even pays child support."

"Harold broke your heart."

"He did, but I got over it," Terri said with a shrug. "We're even still friends, mostly, which is helpful since I see him so often."

"I don't think Jason and I will ever be friends again."

"After the way he treated you, that isn't surprising."

"It wasn't that bad," Camille said after a sip of wine. "He had a mid-life crisis, that's all."

"And he quit his job, left you and your children, and moved into a bug-infested apartment in New York City with his best friend from college so that he could pretend to be twenty-two again."

Camille laughed. "Well, yes, but if I didn't have the children I might be tempted to do the exact same thing."

"But you do have the children and they're his children, too."

"Let's stop talking about our ex-husbands. There must be other things we can talk about."

"We could brag about our wonderful kids, but you already know everything my Thomas is doing. How's Brandon doing with his driving?"

"You know the answer to that. He drove into the most expensive car in Ramsey."

"Maybe Max will forgive him because of your shared past," Terri suggested.

Camille shrugged. "I don't want any favors from the man, but if he did offer to forget about the accident, I'd be grateful. I can't imagine what getting his headlight fixed is going to cost."

"Let's talk about Molly. How is she?" Terri changed the subject.

"She's good. She's training hard, getting ready to test for her black belt."

"Good for her. I keep thinking about signing Thomas up for Tae Kwon Do, but he isn't interested."

"Brandon's been doing it since he was five, but Molly was never interested. I actually had to bribe her to give it a try. She loves it now, though."

"Maybe I should try bribing Thomas, then."

The waiter brought their food and the topic shifted to the weather and what the women were planning to do with the last few days of summer. Camille had walked to the restaurant from home, so she had a second glass of wine while Terri sipped soda.

"And now I suppose I need to go home and make sure the children haven't killed one another," she sighed after she'd scraped up the last of the chocolate icing on her dessert plate.

"Sometimes I'm really happy that I only had one child," Terri told her.

"My two get along really well nearly all of the time, but they do have their moments."

Terri nodded. "And mine complains about being an only child, not all the time, but sometimes."

"Maybe Harold will remarry and have more children."

Terri made a face. "I hope not. I wanted more children, but he didn't, which is one of the reasons why Thomas is an only child. I'd be upset if Harold had more children after not being willing to have any more with me."

"I'm sorry."

"Don't be. It wasn't the only reason and now that I'm on my own with Thomas, I'm grateful he's my only one. I can't see Harold getting married again, anyway. The woman he left me for really broke his heart."

Camille smiled. "Seems only fair."

"There is just a tiny bit of me that feels that he deserved it," Terri told her.

They walked out of the building together. "Let me give you a ride home," Terri said.

"I can walk."

"But I have to drive right past your house."

"Yes, okay, I suppose you do," Camille laughed.

Terri stopped at the exit from the parking lot, carefully looking both ways.

"Wow," she said as a car turned onto the road and then drove past them.

Camille sat back and closed her eyes. "I hope he didn't see me," she said.

Terri laughed. "It's like high school all over again. For what it's worth, I don't think Max even glanced this way. What's interesting is that his headlights were both in perfect working order."

"So he's already had the car repaired," Camille sighed. "I suppose I'll be getting a bill in the mail, then."

"Like I said, maybe he's not going to make you pay since you two were a couple all those years ago."

"He was never the sentimental type," Camille said dryly.

"He was your first boyfriend, wasn't he? I'm trying to remember what you told me about him."

"He was my first boyfriend, yes. We started seeing each other when I was a freshman in high school and we were together until he graduated from college." Camille felt as if she'd been telling the story to everyone lately.

"He's two years older?"

"Yes, he is. He was a junior at the high school when we started dating."

"And you were together for the entire six years?"

"We had a few disagreements, but we never actually broke

up during the six years. In a lot of ways, we grew up together, although he'd had other girlfriends before we started dating."

"So he was your first, but you weren't his," Terri guessed.

Camille felt herself blushing. "He was my first, yes, and he'd already had a good deal of experience before our first time. Maybe not a good deal, actually, but some. I had no idea what I was doing, but he was patient and . . . well, it doesn't matter. I'm sure he's had a lot more experience since then, anyway."

"And you had Jason."

Camille laughed. "Yes, well, let's just not even go there. You can probably pull out now. He's long gone."

"Sorry. I was distracted by the car. I don't really know anything about cars, but that one is seriously sexy."

"So is the driver," Camille muttered.

"I just got a glimpse of him, but he looked pretty good."

"It may not have been Max driving, of course."

"I'm pretty sure it was Max driving. I've seen enough pictures of him over the years."

Camille nodded. "He's always in the news, usually with some stunning blonde or beautiful redhead on his arm."

Terri pulled her car onto the driveway at Camille's house. "Let's do this again before school starts," she suggested.

"Yes, please. Call me and we'll pick out a date."

"Sounds good."

Camille climbed out of the car and let herself into the house, waving to Terri as she shut the door behind herself.

"Mom, Dad wants you to call him," Brandon said as Camille walked into the living room.

"Why?"

"I told him about the accident and he wants to talk to you about it."

Camille sighed. "Did he call you?"

"No, I called him," Brandon said sheepishly. "I know he

and Max Steward used to be friends, so I thought maybe he could persuade Max to forget about the accident. Max can certainly afford to get his own car fixed, after all."

"What did your father say?"

"He said 'Max is back in Ramsey?' and then he said 'Have your mother call me,' and that was it."

She glanced at the clock, hoping it would be too late to make the call, but it was just after eight and she had no excuse, really. She picked up her phone and dialed his number from memory.

"Hello?"

"It's Camille," she said flatly.

"Is Max really back in Ramsey?"

"He is."

"Why?"

"I've no idea."

"What did he say when you talked to him?"

"I haven't spoken to him."

"Well, what did he say when Brandon hit him?" Jason demanded.

"We didn't speak to Max. We talked to his assistant, a man named Seth Pierce."

"Well, when you talk to Max, give him my number, won't you? I'd love to talk to him."

"I can't imagine I'll be talking to him, but if I do, I'll try to remember to give him your number."

"I can't believe Max Steward is back in Ramsey. Of course, he'll just be visiting."

"The rumor is that he's looking to buy the Alexander house."

"Why would he want to do that? Maybe he wants a place to get away from the city once in a while. I suppose Ramsey wouldn't be a bad place for an occasional vacation. You were always obsessed with that old house. Did he know that?"

Camille swallowed hard as she stared out the kitchen window. From where she was standing, she could just see the roof of one of the mansion's towers. It was the view from her bedroom that had inspired all of her childhood dreams. In those days, the house had been occupied, but it had been empty for years now. She didn't want to remember the dozens, maybe hundreds, of hours she'd spent talking with Max about that house.

"Camille? Don't ignore me."

"I'm not ignoring you. I'll tell Max to call you if I ever see him. Was there anything else?" *Are you at all worried about your son having had a car accident, for example,* she added silently.

"I suppose that's all. I may want to come back to Ramsey to see Max, though. I assume I can stay in the spare bedroom."

"You assume incorrectly. If you were coming to see your children, I might consider letting you stay in my house, but since you aren't, perhaps Max can put you up somewhere." Camille put the phone down before Jason could reply. She stood in the kitchen, blinking back tears and breathing slowly, until she was certain she had her emotions in check. Then she rejoined her children in the living room.

They were watching an old movie and she was happy to drop onto the couch between them and let herself get lost in the story.

"What did Dad want?" Brandon asked in a commercial break.

"He wants me to have Max call him if I speak to him."

"If they were such good friends all those years ago, why doesn't he have Max's number?" Brandon asked.

"You'd have to ask your father about that," Camille said.

"Is Dad going to visit before school starts?" Molly asked.

"I don't know. He said something about maybe coming to town, but I don't know if he'll manage it."

"Do we have to clear out the spare room, then?" Molly asked.

The children had turned the spare room into their space. The last time Camille had looked, they had a board game spread across the bed and Brandon's summer homework papers had been on just about every other flat surface.

"He isn't going to stay here if he comes," Camille told them.

"I keep hoping he'll come back," Molly admitted in a low voice.

"I wouldn't let him come back, even if he wanted to," Camille told her. "He left all of us and I would never trust him again, not enough to let him back into our lives in any real way."

The commercials ended before the children replied. Both children were dozing beside her when the credits finally rolled an hour later.

"Off to bed," she told them both. "Brandon, you have to work at one. Molly, we have to go shopping for school supplies tomorrow."

Both children grumbled as they left the room. Camille tucked them up in turn a short while later.

"Oh, I forgot," Brandon exclaimed as Camille switched off his light. "There's a message for you on the answering machine. I heard the phone ringing, but I was in the middle of something on the computer and couldn't get to it in time."

Camille sighed. The children were oddly reluctant to answer the phone when she wasn't home. She went into her bedroom and grabbed the phone off of her nightstand. As she walked into her attached bathroom, she punched the buttons to play the message.

"Camille, it's Max. Call me."

CHAPTER 4

*A*glance at the clock confirmed that it was far too late to return the man's call, even if she'd wanted to do so. She wasn't certain how she felt, though. Max's voice had sent chills through it, but the message itself was abrupt and sounded very much like an order. Some part of her wanted to ignore the call for that reason, but Brandon had hit the man's car. Ignoring his message, no matter how rude, probably wasn't the thing to do.

Her face washed and her teeth brushed, she changed into her pajamas and climbed into bed. *Don't think about Max*, she told herself as she snuggled under the covers. Of course, her brain refused to listen to her and the more she tossed and turned, the more memories of Max tormented her. After an hour, she got up and walked down to the kitchen. A cup of hot chocolate had always been her mother's remedy for insomnia. Camille had never really believed that it worked, but tonight she was willing to try anything.

Whether it was the warm milk in the drink or simply fatigue, Camille managed to fall asleep when she returned to her bed an hour later. She woke up with a headache, feeling exhausted.

"Do we have to go shopping today?" Molly asked over breakfast.

"No, you can go by yourself next week," Camille snapped back. "Take your car and your credit card and get whatever you need."

Molly sighed deeply. "You know I hate back-to-school shopping."

"So do I, and I have to pay for it, as well," Camille pointed out. "You're supposed to be going to Katie's tomorrow, though, and I'm working every day next week. I'm not going shopping over the weekend. The stores will be a nightmare."

"Okay, okay. I'll be ready to go in half an hour," Molly conceded.

Camille nodded. "I just have to make a quick phone call and then we can go." She shut herself in her bedroom and picked up the phone. Max had given her a number that she assumed was for his cell phone. Hoping that she'd get voice mail, she punched in the numbers and held her breath.

"Max Steward." The voice was deep and the words were clipped.

"It's Camille Quinn, returning your call," she said as coolly as she could.

"Camille Quinn," he echoed. "Brandon's mother."

"Yes, that's right."

"Do you have any idea how much it costs to replace a headlight on a car like mine?"

"Twenty-three dollars?" she guessed.

He laughed. "It cost more than that in gas, driving it back to the city for the repair."

"You couldn't get it repaired locally?"

"I didn't even try. I'm certain no one in the area has ever worked on a car like mine."

"Probably not."

"Seth said that you'd prefer not to involve your insurance company in the claim."

"That will depend on what the repairs cost, but Brandon is a new driver and his insurance is already quite expensive."

"As I understand it, he isn't even a licensed driver yet."

"That's correct."

"Which makes you legally responsible for the accident."

"Also correct," Camille replied.

Max chuckled, a sexy sound that sent a shiver down Camille's spine. "I thought maybe we could settle things over dinner tonight, for old times' sake, if nothing else."

"I'm busy tonight," she said quickly. She'd been thinking that he didn't know who she was, but clearly he did.

"Let me make you a better offer, then," Max said. "Have dinner with me tonight and I'll forget that the accident ever happened. Are you less busy now?"

"Sorry, but no, I'm not. I appreciate the offer, but I'm not interested in having dinner with you, not even in exchange for you forgetting the accident happened."

"In that case, I'll put the bill in the mail to you. I see from Brandon's license that you're living in your parents' old house."

"I am. I'll watch for the bill. Sorry about the accident," she said. Feeling as if she might burst into tears, she put the phone down and ended the conversation. In her bathroom, she stared into her mirror.

"Why did he want to have dinner with me?" she demanded.

Her mirror image shook its head.

"Why did I say no?" was her next question.

The woman in the mirror didn't seem to know the answer to that question either.

"I don't want to see him," she explained to herself. "He broke my heart."

"That was thirty-odd years ago," the woman in the mirror said.

"And it still hurts," she said with a deep sigh. She let a single tear slide down her cheek before taking a few deep breaths and blowing her nose. Five minutes later, she found Molly in the kitchen.

"Let's tackle your shopping list, then," she said with artificial cheer. "If we find everything this morning, I'll buy you lunch anywhere you like after we drop Brandon off at work."

"Anywhere?" Molly demanded.

"Anywhere," Camille agreed, knowing that Molly would pick either the Ramsey Inn or the Diner, both of which were fine with her.

"The Diner," Molly said. "I'm craving their chicken."

"Now that you've said that, so am I," Camille laughed. Her head still hurt, but she was determined to ignore it and enjoy her day with her daughter.

"We'll be back at twelve-thirty to take you to work," she told a barely awake Brandon.

"Shurrppsh," he replied.

Camille wrote a large note with the same information and taped it to the refrigerator, secure in the knowledge that Brandon would get hungry and seek out food long before twelve-thirty.

"If you can find everything you want in this store, I'll buy you dessert as well," Camille told her daughter as they walked into the large superstore that was on the edge of the town.

Molly shrugged. "I don't know that they'll have everything, but I'll try."

Ninety minutes later, after a lengthy debate about the relative merits of one planner over another and a last minute change of mind over the appropriate color for a math note-book, the pair were at the checkout.

"That's everything. I get dessert," Molly said happily.

As Camille watched the total mounting, she sighed. "I may have to take a second job to pay for all of this and dessert."

"I don't have to have dessert," Molly said quickly.

"I was teasing," Camille told her. "It was just a joke. We're fine."

"Are you sure? Katie said she thought that we were probably going to have to sell our house to pay for the repairs to Max Steward's car."

Camille frowned. "It was a broken headlight. The car wasn't totaled. Anyway, if it had been, our insurance would cover it."

"Really?"

"Really. You can have school supplies and dessert, but just for today."

Molly laughed. "That's good news because I want apple pie."

"That does sound good," the cashier said. "Maybe I'll join you."

Camille smiled at the woman. "You'd be more than welcome, but you'd have to buy your own pie."

The cashier laughed and pointed to the total on the register. "After paying for this, your credit card is going to need a break."

Molly loaded the bags into the back of the car and then the twosome headed for the Diner.

"I'm glad we finished so quickly. We have time for an early lunch and dessert before we have to get Brandon to work," Camille said as she parked in the small parking lot behind the building.

"And the Diner is always open," Molly added.

It was a real, old-fashioned diner, as well, but the original dining car had been added to over the years. There was still counter seating in the old car, but there were dozens of tables and booths in the large building that opened off of it as well. It was open three hundred and sixty-five days a year and Camille was flooded with memories as she and Molly walked inside.

"Sit anywhere," Sara Snyder, the woman behind the counter, told them. Sara had been working at the Diner for as long as Camille could remember. "The boss is here, though, so pretend I told you to sit somewhere, okay?"

"I heard that," a male voice called from the room at the back. Douglas Holloway stuck his head around the door. Camille didn't know him well, but everyone in Ramsey recognized Lucas Hogan's business manager. Lucas owned at least half a dozen restaurants in the area and Douglas was responsible for managing them on Lucas's behalf.

"Add better soundproofing between the rooms to my wish list," Sara told him.

Douglas chuckled. "But then you'd never hear the customers when they shout out their complaints."

"No one complains in my Diner," Sara shot back.

"That's probably true," Douglas replied.

Camille and Molly took seats on the opposite sides of one of the booths in the back of the room. They glanced over the menu, but they both knew what they wanted.

"We both want the chicken tenders with fries and coleslaw," Camille told Suzy, Sara's daughter and the restaurant's only other full-time employee. "And apple pie for dessert."

"I'll tell Mom. It shouldn't be long," Suzy replied.

True to her word, Suzy delivered the food only a few minutes later. Camille enjoyed every bite of her lunch and her pie.

"Delicious, as always," she told Suzy as the woman cleared their plates. She spoke extra loud, hoping that Douglas, who was sitting a few tables away, would hear her.

"Thanks," Suzy said. "We try hard."

As they headed for the door, Camille stopped. "I'm going to go to the restroom. Do you want to come with me or wait in the car?" she asked Molly.

"I'll wait in the car. I can play on my phone," Molly replied.

Camille handed her the car keys and then turned back around to head for the restrooms in the corner. She was on her way back out when she heard a familiar voice.

"It's good to be back," Max was telling someone.

Camille froze in the doorway between the old diner and the larger restaurant. Max was standing near the diner's entrance talking with Douglas. She took a step backward, sliding into the corner where she hoped she would be out of sight.

"You've been gone for a long time. When I told Lucas you'd come back, he was surprised. Are you planning to stay for long?" Douglas asked.

"I don't have definite plans, but now that I'm here, I'm not certain I'll leave again, actually. I retired on my fiftieth birthday and then I started traveling all over the world, trying to find a place that would feel like home to me. Now that I'm here, I've realized that Ramsey is the only place that truly feels like home."

"I heard you're thinking of buying the Alexander house."

"I'm considering it. It needs a lot of work."

"Lucas and I went around it about a year ago. He was thinking of turning it into a bed and breakfast or a boutique hotel. It needed far too much work, even then. No doubt it's in even worse shape now."

"It's pretty bad, but I can afford to do the repairs. I'm just not sure it's worth the hassle. Land is inexpensive around here. I could buy myself a few acres and build my dream home."

"That would probably be the way to go. It would undoubtably cost less than redoing the Alexander house and you could get exactly what you want."

"I'm not rushing to make any decisions at this point. I'm simply enjoying being home."

"Max? Oh my goodness, Max Steward, it is you," another familiar voice interrupted. "I thought I recognized the car outside and I simply had to stop and say hello."

"Hello," Max replied. To Camille, it sounded as if he had no idea who the woman was.

"You don't even remember me, even though I had a crush on you for all of my high school years," Karen gushed.

"You look far too young to have gone to high school with me," Max told her.

"Oh, you are sweet," Karen replied with a giggle. "I'm Karen Henderson-Archer. I was Karen Henderson back in the day, of course."

"Karen Henderson?" Max repeated. "You were a few years behind me in school, weren't you?"

"I was. I was the same year as Camille Baker and I was unbelievably jealous when you started dating her."

Max laughed. "I wasn't that much of a catch in those days."

"I beg to differ."

"Archer, did you say? Is your husband from Ramsey?"

"Oh, no. I met Donald in college. We settled in Ramsey after he finished medical school."

"I keep bumping into former classmates all over town," Max replied.

"A lot of us came back to raise our own children here. The schools are excellent and Ramsey still feels like a small town where it's safe for kids to play outside until dark. Donald and I have been very happy here."

"That's good to hear."

"Some of our former classmates are more eager to see you than others, of course," Karen added.

"Really?"

"I understand Camille Quinn had her son drive right into you the other night."

Camille frowned. Her mother had always said that when you eavesdrop you never hear anything good about yourself. Clearly, she'd been right.

Max laughed. "It was a minor fender bender and I didn't even recognize Camille at the time."

"She's really looking her age, unfortunately. She was married to Jason Quinn, you know. They had a nice enough life together, even if they did live with Camille's parents. It was such a shame when Jason decided that he'd had enough of being an adult."

"What happened?"

"He quit his job and left Camille and their two kids. Last I heard, he was living in a very nearly condemned apartment in the city with some old college friends, acting as if he were twenty-two again."

"That must be hard on Camille."

"Oh, yes, it is. You can see it in her face. She's working all sorts of hours just to keep a roof over their heads and put food on the table. Teenaged boys eat a lot, too. I'm sure she's glad she has a son and a daughter, instead of two boys."

"Jason doesn't pay child support?"

"I don't think Jason has a job," Karen replied. "I'm sure Camille was hoping that you'd see her at the scene of the accident and fall in love with her all over again. Maybe she was hoping that you'd get blamed for the crash and she could get a small fortune from you."

"Or maybe her son simply misjudged the corner by a few inches and Camille doesn't have any interest in seeing me again."

"She's probably smart enough to realize that you'd never be interested in her now, not after all these years. I've seen the photos of you with supermodels on your arm. Camille can't possibly compete with the sort of women you're used to dating."

"Carefully staged publicity photos have nothing to do with who I am," Max told her.

"Does that mean you're single and looking? Every single woman in Ramsey under the age of ninety will be excited to hear that. Quite a few of the married women might be as well."

"I'm single, but I'm not looking. No need to start working on your divorce," Max replied.

Karen's laugh sounded forced. "Oh, I didn't mean me. Donald and I are deliriously happy together. I even cancelled my vacation so that we could be together."

Camille frowned. She'd forgotten that Karen was meant to be on vacation at the moment. What had happened to all of her plans?

"I'm glad you're happy," Max told her. "And now, if you'll excuse me, I'm sure my food is ready."

"I have everything you ordered here," Sara said loudly. "All packed up to go."

"Thanks," Max replied.

Sara told him how much he owed her.

Max said, "Keep the change," and Camille heard both Suzy and Karen gasp.

"Are you sure?" Sara asked.

"Quite," Max replied.

Camille took a step forward as she heard the diner's door swing open.

"Molly?" Sara said questioningly.

"Mom hasn't come out yet," Molly said in a worried voice.

"She probably ran into an old friend and lost track of time," Sara told her. "Go look for her in the back."

Camille caught her daughter's arm as Molly walked past her. "Don't say anything," she hissed in her ear.

Molly gave her an odd look, but stayed silent. A moment later, Sara spoke again.

"Camille? Max and Karen are both gone."

Blushing brightly, Camille stepped into the diner.

"I could see you on the security cameras," Sara told her. "I figured you should know what people are saying about you, though."

"It was interesting," Camille replied dryly. "But now I'm late for getting Brandon to work."

"What was that all about?" Molly demanded as they climbed into the car.

Not knowing whether she wanted to laugh or cry, Camille repeated the overheard conversations to Molly as she drove them home.

CHAPTER 5

"We're going to go driving after I pick up Brandon," she told Molly several hours later, as she was leaving to pick up her son.

"I'll be here," Molly laughed.

Camille knew that she didn't need to worry about her daughter. Not only was Molly sensible and responsible, they had wonderful neighbors throughout the neighborhood. In an emergency, Molly always had somewhere to go.

"I'm tired and I don't want to drive," Brandon grumbled when he reached the car.

"Drive to Bessie's and I'll buy you ice cream," Camille offered.

Bessie's was a small ice cream stand near the center of town. It was also owned by Lucas Hogan, but Camille had never seen Douglas Holloway at Bessie's. Everyone in town knew that Janet had been running Bessie's for decades, well before Lucas had bought the place and no one wanted him, or anyone else, to make any changes there.

Brandon drove carefully through the streets, heading

straight for the blinking cow sign that advertised the ice cream stand. "Can I have a sundae?"

"You can have whatever you want within reason," Camille replied.

"You bought Molly lunch and dessert," he pointed out.

"This isn't a competition. You don't win anything if I spend more on you today than I did on Molly."

Brandon laughed. "I'll just have the six-scoop sundae, then."

"Six scoops?"

"I'm a growing boy."

"I'm worried about what direction you'll be growing if you keep eating that way, though."

Brandon laughed again and then walked up to the counter and ordered his sundae. "Did you want anything?" he called over his shoulder to Camille.

"I shouldn't, but yes, I want something." She joined him at the counter and ordered herself a two-scoop sundae.

There were a few picnic tables on the grass next to the stand. Camille sat down and took a bite of creamy vanilla ice cream and hot fudge. "Delicious," she sighed.

"It looks as if Max got his car fixed," Brandon said, nodding toward the road behind Camille.

She spun around and then frowned as Max pulled his car into the parking lot for Bessie's. "Oh, no," she exclaimed.

"We could run back to the car," Brandon suggested in a whisper.

"I wish," Camille said, staring at her ice cream and trying to pretend she was invisible.

"He's getting ice cream," Brandon told her a moment later.

Camille nodded and took another bite of her sundae. She barely noticed what she was eating as she waited for Max to leave.

"And here he comes," Brandon warned her a moment later.

"Camille? This is a surprise," Max said. "May I join you?"

Camille glanced around at the other tables. There were four of them and they were all empty. "Sure," she said flatly.

Max chuckled and then slid onto the bench next to her. "Don't sound so pleased to see me," he told her.

"Sorry. Hi, Max, gosh, it's nice to see you again," she said sarcastically.

He raised an eyebrow. "It's a good thing the rest of the town has been more welcoming."

She shrugged and then went back to her ice cream, giving Brandon a look that said "hurry up and eat."

"It's nice to see you again, anyway," Max said after a moment. "You look…"

"Old?" Camille suggested when he trailed off.

"That wasn't at all what I was thinking," Max replied with a laugh. "You actually look almost exactly the way I remember you."

"Don't be fooled by appearances," she warned. "I'm definitely not the same naïve young woman you left behind." She'd been imagining this conversation with Max since she'd first heard that he was back in town. Actually getting to say some of her carefully thought out words was oddly gratifying.

"I should have taken you with me."

Camille forced herself to laugh. "It's all water under the bridge now."

"You married Jason Quinn," he said, sounding as if he couldn't imagine why she would have done so.

"We reconnected at my ten-year reunion," she explained.

"Why was he at your reunion? He graduated two years before you, didn't he?"

Camille nodded, wondering why it mattered. "He actually

came back to Ramsey to go to the reunion with his former girlfriend. Apparently, he'd promised her that he would do that if she didn't have a date."

"Carol Sutton?"

"Yep."

"I'm not clear on how you ended up with Jason, then."

"We talked at the reunion and then he asked me to have dinner with him the next night. Our relationship progressed from there."

"And he moved back to Ramsey to be with you?"

"This is starting to feel like an interrogation."

Max shrugged. "I was just making conversation."

"Tell me about your life, then," Camille suggested. "What's it like coming back here after all of your years in the big city?"

"It's nice," Max said after a moment. "I'd forgotten how nice Ramsey is."

Brandon made a noise. He flushed when Max and Camille looked at him.

"Sorry, Ramsey is nice, it's just boring. I can't wait to go away to college in another two years," he said.

"Don't count on it," Camille warned him.

"Dad wants me to go to New York," Brandon replied.

"And is your father going to pay for you to live there?" she shot back. "I don't want you going deeply in debt to pay for college, not when we have an excellent university right here in town."

"Hailwood is a good school," Max interjected. "It's where I got my degree. You'll have a better chance of making a success of yourself in New York City if you have a degree when you get there."

Brandon shrugged. "We'll see," he muttered.

Scraping up the last of her ice cream, Camille gave Max a

quick smile. "We need to get going," she said. "Brandon has to work in the morning."

"On a Saturday?" Max questioned.

"I'm helping out at a booth at the fair," Brandon told him. "My Tae Kwon Do school always has a booth. It's great for recruiting new students."

"I'll look out for you," Max replied. "I love Ramsey Fair Days."

"You used to love Ramsey Fair Days," Camille corrected him. "You'll find that they've changed a lot since you last attended."

"What's different?" Max asked, looking concerned.

"It's a much bigger event and much more commercial," Camille told him. "You probably remember it as a handful of carnival rides and a few booths selling farm equipment. These days there's an entire midway with rides and games, with booths for just about every local business, and quite a few outside businesses as well. Then there's the food. Bessie's used to have an ice cream truck and one of the local churches would run a bake sale. These days there are dozens of food trucks and other food stands, and dozens of churches, schools, and scouting groups will be selling baked goods."

"Interesting," Max said. "I suppose I was expecting everything to have remained the same here. That was unrealistic of me, of course."

Camille swallowed a dozen replies. "We need to go," she told Brandon.

"I still have an entire scoop to eat," he protested.

"Eat it in the car. I'll drive," Camille replied.

Max put a hand on her arm. "It was nice to see you again," he said softly.

Camille felt herself blushing. "Likewise," she muttered, looking down at the ground.

"You really do look wonderful," he added.

She shrugged. "Don't forget to send me the bill for your car."

"I told you I'd forget all about that if you had dinner with me. I suppose having ice cream together is almost as good."

Camille looked up at him, surprised. "Really?" she asked, hoping he wasn't playing games.

Max stared into her eyes for a moment and then nodded. "Forget about it. It was an accident and it didn't cost that much to get the headlight replaced."

Camille swallowed a lump in her throat and tried to work out how to reply.

"Really?" Brandon asked. "That's wonderful. Thank you so much."

Max turned to look at him. "No problem. Just be a bit more careful next time, okay?"

"I'm being a lot more careful," Brandon promised. "Just look where I parked."

Camille and Max both looked over at the parking lot. Max had parked right in front of Bessie's but Brandon had taken a spot just about as far from the stand as he could possibly be. It was highly unlikely that anyone was going to park anywhere near Camille's car.

"I'll probably see you at the fair," Max said as he stood up.

"I'm not sure I'll be there," Camille replied, busying herself with collecting her bowl, spoon, and napkins. She walked over the large garbage can and dropped everything inside.

"You can't miss the fair," Brandon protested. "You promised to buy me and Molly lunch from the food trucks tomorrow."

Camille shrugged. "We'll see," she said, shooting Brandon a look that she hoped said "be quiet."

"Which food trucks are good?" Max asked.

Brandon launched into a lengthy description of the many

different food trucks that were expected to be serving at the fair. Camille had to force herself not to look at Max. Every time she glanced his way, he seemed to be looking at her. It didn't help that he looked wonderful.

"As much as I hate to interrupt," she said eventually, "we do have to get home."

"Thanks for the tips," Max told Brandon. "I may just have to try a little bit of everything, though."

"You'll be expected to, really, as the town's returning hero," Camille said.

"I'm hardly a hero," Max said quickly. "I'm just a guy who made a few bucks in the city, that's all."

"Everyone thinks you're a billionaire," Brandon interjected. "Ramsey's first ever self-made billionaire."

Max shook his head. "I'm quite a few million short of being a billionaire. I hope the good people of Ramsey won't be too disappointed when they learn that."

"We're just happy you're back," another voice chimed in.

Max turned around and smiled at Janet who'd come out from behind the counter. "It's good to be back."

Janet nodded. "It's like old times, you being here with Camille. The pair of you used to take up my table space for hours at a time, talking and planning your futures."

The words brought tears to Camille's eyes. Janet was right, she and Max had talked a lot about the future over ice cream at Bessie's. It was always a shared future, as well, right up until Max had decided he was leaving.

"We never even bought much," Max said with a laugh. "We'd get a single scoop of ice cream and share it because neither of us had much money."

Janet nodded. "I still get kids who do that, and I still sneak a little extra into every cup. Don't tell that to Douglas Holloway, but this business isn't all about the bottom line profits."

Max grinned. "Some things in Ramsey haven't changed then."

"Your mother must be happy to have you back," Janet suggested.

Camille watched as something flashed over Max's face before he nodded.

"She's always happy to see me," he said.

"How is she? I haven't seen her in years," Janet replied.

"She's good," Max shrugged, gathering up his ice cream bowl and spoon. "She's getting older, of course, and she isn't getting around as much as she used to."

"We're all getting older," Janet laughed. "I'm actually thinking about hiring someone to help out here, although I hate to admit it."

Camille smiled at her. "You should have had help for the last twenty or thirty years. Bessie's is a lot of work for one person."

"It's all I've ever done. I started working here part-time, when I was in high school. Once I'd graduated, the owner started giving me more hours until I was the only one here whenever the stand was open. He sold the place to Lucas Hogan some ten years ago and he had my job written into the sales agreement. I suppose one day, in another twenty or thirty years, I'll simply drop dead behind the counter."

"You should retire and travel the world," Brandon suggested.

"That's a dream for a young person. I have no interest in traveling. I have everything I need here in Ramsey. I don't know what I'd do with myself if I retired, either. I love my job, but I wouldn't mind a bit of help with moving boxes and with cleaning behind the freezers, that sort of thing."

"You need to have a talk with Douglas," Camille suggested.

Janet made a face. "I suppose I should, but he's hard to

talk to. He's only interested in making money for Lucas. He doesn't appreciate what Bessie's means to the community." She looked around at all of the empty tables and sighed. "Then again, maybe he's right. Maybe the community doesn't appreciate Bessie's anymore, either."

"Don't say that," Camille exclaimed. "Bessie's is a Ramsey institution."

Janet nodded, but she didn't look convinced.

"I can't imagine why you aren't busy," Max said. "That was some of the best ice cream I've had in years."

"I still make it all myself from the recipes the original owner gave me," Janet told him. "I can tell you why we aren't busy, though. There's a fancy new place on the other side of town that does frozen yogurt with what seems like a thousand different toppings. That's much more appealing for young people, it seems."

"It's good," Brandon told her. "But not as good as your ice cream."

"But it has indoor seating and it's open later," Camille added.

"I have to close when it gets dark, otherwise, the lights attract bugs," Janet replied.

"Well, now that I'm home, I'll be stopping in for ice cream regularly," Max told her.

"Bring your mother once in a while," Janet suggested.

Max smiled but it looked forced to Camille. "I should do that," he said.

"Thanks again for forgetting about the accident," Brandon said as he threw away his empty ice cream bowl. "I really appreciate it."

"Not a problem. I'm sure I'll see you at the fair tomorrow," Max replied. "Maybe you, too," he said to Camille.

She turned her head away as she felt herself blushing. "Yeah, maybe," she muttered as she headed for her car.

"I can drive," Brandon said when they reached the vehicle. "I'll just wait until Max has gone."

"Must you?" Camille asked, unable to stop staring at Max as he said something to Janet.

"I don't want to be anywhere near his car," Brandon explained.

"Just drive," Camille said as Max pulled Janet into a hug.

Brandon started the car and pulled very slowly and carefully out of the parking lot. "Max was really nice," he said after a moment.

"Yeah, great," Camille replied.

"He isn't going to make me pay for his headlight."

"That was kind of him," Camille admitted. "Although, he can certainly afford to be generous."

"Was it weird, seeing him again?"

"Weird? I'm not sure that's the right word. We didn't exactly part on good terms. I know it was thirty-something years ago, but there's a part of me that's still angry at him, I think."

"Thirty years is a long time to be angry at someone."

"It is, yes," Camille replied. There was no point in trying to explain to Brandon how badly Max had hurt her. It was all ancient history anyway. She was grateful to Max for dropping the accident claim, but it would probably be for the best if she never saw the man again, she decided.

"What time do you have to be at the fair tomorrow?" she asked Brandon when she checked on him before bed.

"Nine, although Master Caldwell said eight-thirty would be better if we can drag ourselves out of bed that early."

"I'll drag you out of bed," Camille laughed.

HER ALARM WENT off at seven the next morning. "Saturdays are supposed to be for sleeping in," she groaned as she rolled out of bed. In truth, she hadn't slept in on a Saturday in years. One or the other of her children usually had something they wanted or needed to do on a Saturday morning. On the rare Saturdays when she didn't have to take the children anywhere, she was always happy to get up and get laundry done or get to the grocery store.

She woke both kids and then took a shower, humming to herself as she washed her hair. Ramsey Fair Days had become bigger and more commercial, but she was almost as excited about them now as she had been when she'd been younger. The event brought just about everyone in the small town together. There would be wonderful food, some of it only available during the fair, booths full of information about everything from remodeling her home to buying a boat or a recreational vehicle, and just about everywhere she'd turn, she would run into a friend.

"Katie is going to meet us there," Molly told her as they all got into the car. "She was just getting up when I texted her."

"She'll miss the best part," Camille laughed.

The fair's grand opening celebration would be held around ten o'clock. The local government officials would be there, along with dozens of invited guests and every newspaper and television reporter the town could muster up. Camille much preferred the earlier and unofficial opening of the fair. At nine, Trevor Harrison, the town's oldest living resident, would unlock the gates that had been locked during the closing ceremony at the end of last year's fair. Then the gates would be slid back and Trevor would announce that the fair was now open.

Only a handful of people attended the unofficial opening, but for Camille, it was the only opening that mattered. Of course, the gates that Trevor unlocked weren't used for anything other than the ceremony and the fairgrounds were used for dozens of other events during the year, but none of that mattered to Camille. Trevor would also play a part in the official opening, but Camille had no interest in watching that. Her parents had always taken her to the nine o'clock ceremony and she'd continued that tradition with her own children. It was probably silly, but it mattered to her.

CHAPTER 6

At eight-thirty, Camille turned Brandon over to Master Caldwell and then she and Molly headed for the gates at the back of the fairgrounds.

"Katie is going to meet us at the old gates," Molly told her after her phone buzzed. "She's never seen the unofficial opening ceremony."

"I'm surprised they keep having it, really. My mother told me that when she was a child the gates were actually kept locked between fairs and this ceremony was the official one, but over time things changed."

"I hope they don't ever stop doing this one. It's an important Ramsey tradition," Molly said.

"Only to a handful of people," Camille said, gesturing toward the dozen or so men and women who were gathered near the locked gates.

"It means a great deal to Trevor, though," a woman standing nearby said. "He takes great pride in keeping the keys between fairs." Camille recognized Clare Munroe who'd once been a teacher at the town's elementary school. Clare was around seventy-five and Camille knew that she fancied herself as the town's unofficial historian.

Camille nodded. "His mother always enjoyed the fair. She unlocked the gates for many, many years."

"She was the last of the Ramseys, of course," Clare said. "It's a shame her brother passed away before he could have children."

"Trevor is a Ramsey in everything but name," Camille argued.

"And his son is a Ramsey," Molly interjected.

"I suppose he'll be here today," Clare replied. "Ramsey Harrison, I mean. I wonder how many wives he's had now."

"I believe he's married to his fifth," another voice supplied.

Camille felt herself blushing as she recognized Max's voice. She took a deep breath and deliberately didn't turn around to acknowledge the man.

"Five?" Clare snapped. "It simply isn't right."

"It simply isn't any of our business," Max said smoothly. "Good morning, everyone."

"Good morning," Molly said. "I'm Molly Quinn."

"Ah, yes, Brandon's sister," Max replied. "It's very nice to meet you."

"I didn't realize you and Max were together again," Clare said to Camille in a loud whisper

"We aren't," she replied flatly.

"Looks like it," Clare said with a shrug. "You should have brought your mother," she said to Max.

"She wasn't feeling her best this morning. I may bring her tomorrow, if she's up to it," Max replied easily.

"Good morning," another voice said.

Camille turned and smiled at Seth Pierce. "Good morning," she said brightly. "Welcome to Ramsey Fair Days."

"Thank you. I'm rather looking forward to all of this. I

grew up in a succession of big cities. I've never been to a town fair before."

"Who are you?" Clare demanded.

Seth laughed and then crossed to stand right next to the woman. "I'm Seth Pierce. I'm one of Max's assistants. I'll bet you're the perfect person to tell me all about the fair."

Clare shrugged. As she began to share the fair's history with Seth, he started to slowly lead her away from Max. Camille watched until they were several feet away.

"I didn't realize his job description included chasing people away from you," she said to Max.

He shrugged. "He's truly interested in the history of the fair, but he knows I don't want to hear about it. I had Miss Sutton as a first grade teacher, after all."

"Didn't we all?" Camille replied.

"I didn't," Molly said.

"No, she finally retired about ten years ago," Camille agreed. "Your brother had her, though."

Molly nodded. "He didn't like her," she told Max.

"Good morning," a voice said. Several of the town's officials had gathered in front of the gates. Now they began the simple ceremony that Camille had enjoyed every year since her childhood.

"We're delighted to have our town's oldest living resident here today to officially open Ramsey Fair Days," one of the men said. "Trevor, we're glad you could be here today."

Trevor was sitting in a wheelchair a few feet away. For a moment, Camille was worried that he'd fallen asleep, but when the man behind the chair touched his arm, Trevor sat up and then slowly rose to his feet.

"I'm glad to be here for another fair," he said in a slightly shaky voice. The man behind the chair stepped forward and offered Trevor his arm. Together they took the handful of steps needed to get to the gates. "My son, Ramsey," Trevor told the crowd.

Camille studied Ramsey, who had to be in his mid-seventies. The family had a history of longevity so she wasn't surprised to see that he looked younger and healthier than his years might suggest. He smiled out at the crowd.

"That's my guy," a woman standing near Max said, waving at Ramsey.

The woman appeared to be at least thirty years younger than Ramsey. She was wearing a short sundress and very high heels. Her hair was bleached blonde, and her lipstick was bright red.

"Congratulations," Max told her.

She flushed. "Thanks. We've only been together for a few weeks. Technically, he's still married to someone else, but he's getting that sorted out."

The noise that Clare made was audible throughout the area. Ramsey waved a hand.

"Let's just get on with things, shall we?" he asked.

"Where are the keys, then?" Trevor demanded.

"I thought you had them," Ramsey shot back.

Trevor began patting his pockets.

"What happens if he can't find them?" Max whispered to Camille.

"Oh, he does this every year. He always finds them, but he likes to make us wait," she replied.

After another minute, Trevor pulled a key ring out of his pocket. He held it up triumphantly. "I knew they were here somewhere," he announced.

Ramsey helped his father shuffle forward another foot and then held the gates steady while Trevor turned the key. "I declare that the Ramsey Fair is now open," Trevor announced.

The crowd applauded politely and then began to disperse as Ramsey helped his father back into his wheelchair.

"Thank you all for attending," one of the suited men said loudly. "The official opening of the fair will take place at the grandstand at ten o'clock. I hope to see you all there."

"I'd better go and get a seat," Clare said. "I'm so happy that you and Max are back together again," she told Camille before she turned and rushed away.

Camille swallowed a sigh. "We aren't," she muttered under her breath.

"I missed it, didn't I?" Katie demanded as she rushed up to Molly. "Dad couldn't find anywhere to park, well, not anywhere close by. We ended up having to walk for ages and then I wasn't sure where the ceremony actually took place. You weren't answering your phone, either."

"I turned the sound off during the ceremony," Molly explained. "I recorded it, though, so you can see what you missed."

The two girls huddled under the shade of a large tree so that Katie could watch the video.

"She's beautiful," Max said in a low voice.

"Thank you. I think she looks too much like me."

"She reminds me of your mother, actually, but she does look like you, as well."

"She and Mom were very close. We both miss her a lot."

"I'm sorry for your loss. I was in Europe when she passed and I didn't hear about it until after I was home. I would have sent flowers otherwise."

Camille shrugged. "We had a lot of flowers. They didn't help."

He nodded. "My mother isn't well but I'm not letting myself think about what might happen if she passes."

"I'm sorry. It's never easy to lose a parent."

"Your father is gone, as well, isn't he?" Max asked.

"He passed away around six years ago. His death was harder on Brandon than Molly."

"And then Jason left?"

"I think my father's death was a part of that. Jason was suddenly confronted by his own mortality. He started making a bucket list the day after my father's funeral. By the following week, he'd realized that the only way he'd ever accomplish everything on it was if he left me and the kids and dedicated the rest of his life to the items on the list."

"What a selfish thing to do."

"You'd know all about that," Camille replied.

Max flushed. "Touché."

"I'm sorry, Mrs. Quinn, but that wasn't very exciting," Katie said as she and Molly walked over and joined them.

"It isn't meant to be exciting," Camille told her. "The official ceremony is the exciting one. I believe there are even going to be fireworks and drones this year."

Katie rolled her eyes. "It will be lame. It's always lame."

Camille laughed. "They try hard."

"They'd be better off using the money for something more important," Molly said. "Teacher salaries or college scholarships, maybe."

"The fair brings a lot of visitors into the town," Camille told her. "Our hotels, restaurants, and other businesses all benefit. Then they pay more in taxes and that benefits the schools."

"Whatever," Molly replied.

Max laughed. "Your mother is right. The fair does a lot of good for the town. Anyway, the fireworks and special effects at the opening ceremony have all been donated this year by a benefactor."

"Really?" Camille asked. "Anyone you know?"

"That would be telling," he replied.

"Max, they're waiting for you at the grandstand," Seth interrupted.

After a glance at the expensive-looking watch on his wrist, Max frowned. "Is it too late to get out of going?" he asked.

Seth sighed. "You know what I'm going to say."

"I do," Max replied. "Camille, Molly, Katie, would you care to join me in the grandstand for the official opening of the fair?"

"Oh, can we?" Molly asked excitedly. "No one I know ever gets to sit in the grandstand."

"Karly Archer sits there every year," Katie countered. "Her father buys a whole row of seats."

"Yes, but I don't actually know Karly Archer. She's two years older and two million dollars richer," Molly shot back.

"I don't think she has two million dollars," Katie laughed.

"I don't think sitting in the grandstand is a good idea," Camille said to Max.

"Why not?" he asked her as the two girls protested.

"People are already accusing me of doing everything I can to win you back. I'd rather not add fuel to the fire."

"I don't much care what people say about me," Max replied with a shrug.

"That's because once things get unbearable, you can simply hop into your fancy car and drive away, leaving me to live with everyone talking about me and giving me sympathetic looks for the next five years," she snapped.

Max looked stunned. "Was it that bad?"

"You can't even begin to imagine," she told him flatly.

"I never meant to hurt you," he began.

She held up a hand. "Let's just agree not to ever have that conversation. I'd rather we didn't ever have any conversations, actually."

"Can the girls sit with me, then? They'd really like to and I don't want to sit there with just Seth."

Camille shook her head. "I think it would be best…"

"Mom, please?" Molly interrupted. "You and Max can sit on opposite ends of the row and ignore each other for the entire ceremony, but this is a once in a lifetime opportunity for me and Katie."

"Katie just said it was going to be lame, remember?" Camille replied.

"It will be far less lame from the grandstand," Katie told her.

"You can sit next to Seth," Max offered. "Everyone will assume you're dating him."

Seth grinned. "I should be so lucky." He offered his arm. "Shall we?" he asked.

"Please?" Molly and Katie said together.

Sighing, Camille took Seth's arm and let him lead her to the grandstand. Molly and Katie bounced along excitedly behind them. Max followed, an amused look on his face.

A woman wearing a business suit and a frown met them at the entrance to the grandstand. "Mr. Steward? Right this way, please," she said. Spinning on her heel, she led them up the stairs to a row near the top. "This is your section," she told Max. "If you want anything, drinks or snacks, just let me know."

"Anyone want a drink or a snack?" Max asked the girls.

Molly looked at her mother and then slowly shook her head. Katie grinned. "Cotton candy?" she asked.

"Of course," the woman replied. "Just one?"

"You can have some, too, but then that's it until after lunch," Camille told her daughter.

"Two cotton candies, please," Molly said happily.

"Camille? Do you want a drink or anything?" Max asked.

"I'm fine," Camille muttered. She rarely drank, but a glass

of wine suddenly sounded incredibly good. It was far too early in the morning for any such thing, of course, she reminded herself as she followed Seth down the row. As she dropped into a seat, Max slid into the seat next to her.

"If you really want me to, I'll move," he told her.

"People are going to talk," she reminded him.

"They're already talking about me. I suppose I'd rather they were talking about us getting back together than anything else."

"Except we aren't getting back together," she reminded him.

He smiled and then gestured toward the stage below them. "I think they're ready to start."

Several large bags of cotton candy were delivered as the first official began to speak. Camille found herself holding one on her lap as the ceremony continued.

"You look as if you're trying to hide behind that," Max whispered during a lull.

"I might be."

He sighed. "Most women would be happy to have their names connected to mine."

"I'm not most women."

"No, you aren't."

Camille did her best to ignore the man sitting next to her, trying to focus on the ceremony below them. It had been over thirty years since she'd been this close to the man and it was nothing but annoying the way her body seemed to be responding to him. As he crossed his arms and his fingers brushed up her forearm, she felt a rush of electricity follow his touch.

The urge to reach out and take his hand was almost overwhelming. To distract herself, she opened the bag of cotton candy and pulled out a handful. There was no way she was going to touch him with sticky fingers, she thought to herself. A moment later, Max reached into the bag and grabbed a handful of the sweet treat.

"I hope you don't mind," he whispered.

"Help yourself," she replied.

The next time she reached into the bag, he did the same. As their fingers connected, she pulled her hand away, sending a cloud of cotton candy into the air.

Max chuckled. "You have cotton candy in your hair," he said softly.

She didn't breathe as he carefully removed bits of spun sugar from her hair, her forehead, and then from her cheek.

"Max, it's time for your bit," Seth hissed from Camille's other side.

He looked over at his assistant and then sighed. "Duty calls," he told Camille before he stood up and slowly walked down to the stage as the crowd clapped and cheered.

"I'm delighted to be back home in Ramsey," Max said into the microphone. "I'm excited to announce what will be the first of many charitable initiatives that I'll be spearheading now that I'm back. The Ramsey Fair Days Fund will provide a pool of money that will pay at least a portion of the participation costs for the various non-profit groups that take part in the fair. More details will be forthcoming in the weeks and months ahead as to how the fund will support the fair in the years to come, but for this year, I'm pleased to announce that it will be paying the participation fees in full for every non-profit that has a booth or a table at the fair."

The crowd cheered. Camille sighed. Max's gesture was very generous and she was happy for the non-profit groups who would benefit, but just because the whole town loved him didn't mean that she had to forgive him.

"And now, I believe we have fireworks and drones or something," Max laughed. He pushed a button on the podium and the first loud bang sounded. The high school band began to play a lively tune that was accompanied by the promised fireworks. A pair of drones flew overhead, but as Max made his way back to his seat, one of them disappeared out of sight behind a large tree.

"Drones might have been a bit ambitious," Max whispered as he sat back down.

"Duck," Camille told him as the second drone veered off course and then crashed into the stage.

Max chuckled. "I hope they weren't aiming for me."

The drone began to smoke and then started a small fire. Someone rushed onto the stage with a fire extinguisher to put out the blaze as the band played on and the fireworks continued to explode.

A few minutes later, an official approached the podium. "That was quite the show," he said, wiping his brow with a handkerchief. "And now, Trevor Harrison will officially open the fair."

Ramsey led his father forward to the podium. Trevor looked out at the crowd.

"I haven't got anything that can follow that," he said after a moment. "The fair is open."

The crowd laughed and applauded and then began to spread out across the fairgrounds.

"What's fun at the fair, then?" Max asked Molly and Katie.

"The rides," they replied together.

"Let's go," Max said with a wicked grin that made Camille's heart skip a beat.

CHAPTER 7

"To keep people from talking, you should probably ride with Seth," Max told Camille as they walked through the fairgrounds.

"I don't ride," she replied.

"You used to love the rides," Max exclaimed.

"That was thirty years ago. I got older and had two children. Now I get sick to my stomach on the carousel."

Max frowned. "I haven't been on fair rides in thirty years. I hope I can still manage them."

"Start with the easier rides, just in case," Camille suggested.

He nodded. "Are you sure you can't do the carousel?"

She shrugged. "I haven't actually tried riding it in years."

Max insisted on paying for a huge book of tickets, far more than Camille thought they would ever use.

"Let's start with the carousel and see how it goes," he said as he rejoined the group, tickets in hand.

"Mom never rides anything," Molly told him.

"Mom is going to try to carousel this year," Camille interjected. "That may well be the only thing I ride, but I used to love everything."

It was still fairly early and the group had almost the entire ride to themselves. Camille selected a white horse, one that wouldn't move up and down as the ride rotated. Max jumped on the horse next to hers while Molly and Katie found horses they liked nearby. Seth shrugged and climbed onto a horse near Max. The music started and Camille had to blink back a rush of tears as the carousel began to move.

A jumble of memories had her shaking her head as she recalled riding as a small child, her father standing beside her; riding repeatedly for hours when one of her high school friends was in charge of taking tickets; and then riding with Max, year after year, holding hands across the gap between the horses. The last time she'd ridden, she'd been pregnant with Brandon and she'd ended up having to leave the fair after a single ride because it had left her feeling so unwell.

As the horses made their slow progress to nowhere, Camille found that she was enjoying herself. Molly and Katie were laughing together in front of her and if she ignored Max, she could almost pretend that she was simply having a fun day out with her kids. She'd have to get some ride tickets for Brandon later, she thought. He'd want to ride a few things once he was finished working.

The music stopped and the ride gradually slowed. It took Camille a minute to work out how to climb off the horse.

"Need a hand?" Max asked. He moved into the gap between the horses, much too close for Camille's comfort.

"I'm fine," she said quickly, swinging her leg so that she could get off on the opposite side of the animal. Her foot caught on the leather strap that could be used as a seatbelt for smaller children. She lost her balance and very nearly fell head first onto the ground below.

"Steady there," Max said in her ear as he slid his arms around her, righting her and then helping her climb down.

"Thanks," she muttered. As soon as her feet were on the ground, she took several quick steps away from the man. He didn't say as word as she blushed and turned away.

"Mom, are you okay?" Molly asked.

"I'm fine. I just lost my balance for a second," Camille told her.

"What next?" Molly demanded.

"Maybe I'll skip the next one," Camille replied.

"Are you feeling sick?" Molly wanted to know.

"Actually, I feel pretty good," Camille admitted. "But that doesn't mean I want to ride anything else."

"How about the Ferris wheel?" Molly asked. "We can probably see our house from up there."

Camille nodded. "You can see all of Ramsey from the top, or at least, you used to be able to see all of Ramsey. The town might be a bit bigger now than it used to be, though."

"I don't remember looking at the view on the Ferris wheel when we rode," Max said in a low voice as the group made their way to the ride.

Camille blushed. The small cars of the Ferris wheel had given the young couple some time alone together. Max was right. In those days, they'd paid no attention to the view.

"The cars were smaller in our day," Max laughed as the entire group was able to fit into a car together.

"It wasn't as high, either," Camille said, feeling slightly worried as they began to climb.

"But look at the view," Katie exclaimed. "I can see my house over there."

Camille looked down and swallowed hard as a wave of vertigo washed over her. She shut her eyes and then opened them again slowly.

"There's our house," Molly said excitedly.

"And your creepy neighbor's house," Katie added.

"The Alexander house isn't creepy," Camille told her. "It's just very old and in need of repairs."

From where she was sitting, Camille had to admit that the huge old house did seem to resemble a haunted house. There were towers and spires and the entire building looked neglected and sad.

"It's a beautiful building," Max said with a sigh. "I can't decide if it's worth sinking a fortune into or not, though."

"We'd be neighbors," Molly laughed.

"There is that," Max said, winking at Camille.

She blushed and then returned her gaze to the town below them. The ride had stopped as riders were being loaded into the empty car opposite theirs.

"I can see your old house," she told Max a moment later.

He leaned over and looked where she was pointing. "It needs a new roof," he said. "Mom won't hear of it, though. She doesn't want anything done to her home."

"I can't see why she'd object to a new roof," Camille replied.

"She doesn't want the hassle and the noise, mostly. I could probably talk her into it, but then I'd have to deal with her being upset the whole time the work was being done."

"Take her away for a weekend and have it done while you're gone," Camille suggested.

"It's a good idea, but sadly not possible," he said.

Camille glanced at him. The look on his face told her to stop asking questions. "There's the high school," she said as she looked away.

The girls weren't excited to see the school, but then the ride began to move again. They went around a second time before their turn ended.

"How about the crazy mouse?" Katie asked.

"That's too much for me," Camille said quickly. "You guys can ride, though."

"Mr. Steward, do you want to ride it?" Molly asked.

"Call me Max, and yes, I do," he laughed.

"I'm going to sit this one out," Seth said quickly. He hadn't looked happy on the Ferris wheel, so Camille wasn't surprised.

"Are you okay?" she asked him as Max and the girls walked away.

"Just a bit queasy, but I'm sure it will pass. I didn't realize that riding carnival rides was going to be in my job description," he replied.

"Don't ride anything else. I'll get you some ginger ale. That might help."

"I'm fine. I just need to sit down for a few minutes," he countered.

There were benches dotted around just about everywhere. They found one in a shady corner and sat down together.

"How long have you been working for Max, then?" Camille asked after a while.

"Almost two years. I was working as an assistant to the CEO of one of the largest banks in the US when I met him. He talked me into coming to work for him."

"And you still work for him, even though he's retired."

"He's retired, but I'm not," Seth laughed. "I'm working harder now than I ever did before Max retired, doing my best to keep up with the man."

Dozens of questions sprang into Camille's head, but she didn't want to ask any of them. The last thing she wanted was for anyone to think that she was interested in Max.

"Where are you from originally?" was the question she finally asked.

"I grew up outside of Boston, in one of the smaller

suburbs. I went to college in New England, as well, and then moved to New York City."

"And did you like the city?"

"I loved New York. Then again, I loved Boston, too. I'm a big city person."

"Ramsey must be something of a shock for you, then."

He chuckled. "It's been odd, but interesting, being here. I can't imagine I'll stay much longer. Max will either decide to actually retire, in which case he won't need me, or he'll decide that we should go back to the city."

"Which is more likely?" Camille blurted out before she could stop herself.

"I wish I knew," Seth sighed.

"Camille? I didn't realize you had a new man in your life," a voice said.

Camille forced herself to smile as Karen Henderson-Archer stared curiously at Seth. "Karen, this is Seth Pierce. He's Max's assistant," Camille explained.

"Max's assistant? Does that mean that Max is here some-where?" Karen replied, running her fingers through her hair and licking her lips.

"He's on the crazy mouse with Molly and Katie," Camille replied.

"Junior and Karly are planning to ride everything. I wonder if they've crossed paths yet," Karen said, looking around.

"You aren't riding?" Camille asked.

Karen flushed and then shrugged. "I haven't ridden in years, but maybe I'm missing out. Maybe I should ride with Max on a few things." .

"I'm sure he'd love that," Camille said. She could feel Seth suppressing a laugh, but Karen didn't seem to notice.

"I should go and find them," Karen said excitedly.

"As I said, they were heading for the mouse. They can't have gone far," Camille replied.

Karen nodded and then turned and walked away.

"I should follow her. Part of my job is keeping people like her away from Max," Seth said as they watched her go.

"Max might enjoy having someone to ride with," Camille suggested.

"Someone, maybe, but not her. She keeps bumping into Max all over town and every time she sees him, she drops hints that they should get together."

"Max might be misunderstanding her, actually. As far as I know, she's very happily married," Camille protested.

Seth shrugged. "I don't think Max is misunderstanding anything, but he knows she's married and he isn't interested."

"Maybe we should go and find Max and warn him," Camille sighed. "Are you feeling better?"

"I am, actually, but I'm not going on any more rides," he said firmly.

"That makes two of us," Camille laughed.

They hadn't gone far before they spotted Max, Molly, and Katie. They were deep in conversation as Camille and Seth approached.

"...before we try anything a second time," Molly was saying.

"But the lines are short for the mouse right now," Katie argued.

"Let's do one other ride and then the mouse again," Max suggested. "Then we'll see how we feel."

"Karen is looking for you," Camille told Max.

"Karen Archer?" he asked, making a face.

"She thought maybe you'd like to ride with her," Camille replied.

"Are you sure you don't want to ride anything else?" Max asked a bit desperately.

"Max! There you are," Karen's shrill voice cut through the morning air. She came rushing toward them, dragging her children along with her.

"Max, these are my entire reason for being," she beamed when she reached them. "This is Donald, Junior. We call him Junior. And this is Karly, my mini-me."

Karly frowned and then shook her head. "I'm nothing like my mother," she said in a dull voice. "I don't even look like her."

That was certainly true at the moment, as Karly had chopped off her long blonde hair and dyed what was left purple with green stripes. She was wearing colored contact lenses that made her eyes bright purple and she'd accented everything with black lipstick.

Karen laughed. "Well, you certainly don't look like your father," she said.

Her son looked at her and raised an eyebrow. "Not sure you should be saying that too loudly," he told his mother.

Karen flushed. "Anyway, we heard you were riding the rides and we thought we might join in the fun," she told Max.

"Sure," he replied with a shrug. "We were just about to go on the flying swings."

"Cool," Junior said.

"Flying swings?" Karen repeated, looking uncertain.

"Mom, just wait here. I'm sure Camille isn't riding," Karly snapped.

"I'm not," Camille agreed, trying not to sound as amused by the entire situation as she actually was.

"Oh, no. I'll ride," Karen insisted. "It will be fun."

Karly rolled her eyes and then turned and stomped off toward the swings. As the others followed, Karen took Max's arm.

"I haven't ridden anything in years," she told him. "You may need to hold my hand while we're riding."

"I'm looking after the girls because Camille can't ride," Max said, sounding apologetic. "Seth can hold your hand, though."

Karen glanced back at Seth and for a moment Camille thought she was tempted.

"Oh, no," Seth muttered.

When they reached the swings, Camille noted that there were three swings in each row. If Max sat between the girls, Karen could sit between her own children, which made perfect sense. No doubt Karen wouldn't see it that way.

"The girls should all sit together," Karen said as they joined the end of the line. "Karly, you can sit in the middle and keep an eye on Megan and Kathy."

"It's Molly and Katie," Max corrected her. "And I'll be sitting between them. You can sit with your children."

"Must she?" Karly drawled.

Karen laughed nervously. "It's going to be such fun," she said, sounding as if she was simply trying to persuade herself.

"It's going to be fun for the spectators, anyway," Seth laughed as the group of riders made their way to the swings. He and Camille found a bench across from the ride and settled in.

"And they're off," Camille said as the swings began a slow revolution. A few seconds later, they were spinning rapidly and getting higher and higher.

"Just watching is making me feel sick," Seth admitted.

"You'd have to pay me a fortune to get me on that," Camille replied.

"How much?" Seth asked. "I'm not offering or anything, I'm just curious."

Camille thought about it for a moment. "Enough to fix up my house and put my kids through college, maybe. Oh, who am I kidding? I'd do it for a lot less than that. Ten grand, maybe."

"It would take at least a hundred thousand to get me on that ride," Seth announced as the swings began their descent. "Two hundred thousand if they're actually going to start it up while I'm on it."

Camille laughed. "Karen doesn't seem to have had fun," she remarked as the swings stopped and she watched the other woman stagger off the ride.

As soon as she was clear of the swings, Karen stopped and finger combed her hair. Then she took a deep breath and straightened her shoulders before she marched away from the ride to join everyone at the bench where Camille and Seth were waiting.

"What fun," Karen said in an artificially bright voice. "What's next?"

"Crazy mouse," Katie told her. "Max said we could do it again after the swings."

"You don't have to ride," Junior told his mother.

"Oh, no, I want to ride," Karen protested. "I haven't been on the crazy mouse since high school."

"Let's go," Max said.

"Let's follow," Seth said as the group moved away. "I don't want to miss this."

Camille laughed and then she and Seth followed the others at a more leisurely pace.

"Karen is going to insist on riding with Max," Camille predicted.

"He may even agree so that the kids can ride together," Seth replied with a shrug.

"Poor Max," Camille whispered.

When they got to the front of the line, Camille could see them debating about the pairings. After an awkward moment, Max and Karen climbed into a car together. Camille was sure she saw a triumphant smile on Karen's face as she snuggled into the tight seat with Max.

Molly and Katie both waved at her as the ride pulled away from the platform. As the cars raced down the track, Camille felt as if she could see the color draining out of Karen's face. The train went around once and then stopped at the station. After a short pause, it started up again, this time running backwards along the same track. After another stop at the station, it raced around forwards again.

Max had to help Karen climb out of the car when it finally stopped for good. She was swaying and looked slightly green.

"That was great," she said as they joined Seth and Camille. "Such good fun."

"You don't look as if you feel well," Seth told her.

"I'm fine," Karen snapped. "I could do this all day."

"Let's do it again, then," Karly suggested.

Karen smiled faintly and then took a deep breath. "Maybe I should sit this one out," she said.

"Camille can ride with Max this time," Seth said.

Karen frowned. "Then again…" she began. Before she could finish her sentence, her eyes went wide and she took a step backwards. As everyone watched, she ran to the nearest garbage can and began to throw up.

"I don't know her," Karly said with a sigh.

"She just overdid it after years of not riding," Camille said. "You guys go and have fun. I'll look after her while you ride a few more things."

"Are you sure?" Junior asked. His sister was dragging him away before Camille could reply.

"Are you sure?" Max asked, looking from Camille to Karen and back again.

"I'm sure. You go and have fun with the girls. I'll be here somewhere," she told him.

"What can I do?" Seth asked.

"Get some ginger ale from one of the stands please, and some ice and paper towels might help, too."

He nodded and then rushed away while Camille headed toward Karen who was still leaning over the garbage can.

CHAPTER 8

"*A*re you okay?" Camille asked Karen when she reached her.

Karen looked up with tears in her eyes. "I think Donald is having an affair," she blurted out.

Camille swallowed a dozen replies. "I'm sorry," was what she finally settled on.

"I canceled my trip to try to save my marriage, but Donald keeps telling me that I'm imagining things and that our marriage is fine."

"What do you want?" Camille asked, not certain she wanted to hear the answer.

Karen shrugged. "I don't know. I don't want to talk about it."

Camille nodded. "Are you feeling less sick now?" she asked, wording the question carefully.

"There's nothing left in my stomach now," Karen replied. "I just wanted to feel like I was eighteen again, that's all. I hate that I'm fifty and that I can't still do all the things that I did when I was younger."

You're fifty-one, Camille thought but didn't say. "I blame my children," she said instead. "Being pregnant and giving birth messed up my entire system."

Karen nodded. "My body has never properly recovered from having my two. I suppose I shouldn't blame Donald for wanting to sleep with a younger woman who's never had kids."

"I very much doubt that his body still looks like it did when he was nineteen," Camille said dryly.

Karen gave her a weak smile. "He works hard to stay in shape, but his age is definitely showing. I work hard, too, but clearly not hard enough."

"I have some experience with men and mid-life crises," Camille reminded her.

"Yes, and at least Donald hasn't left me. He'll get tired of his fling and come back to me. He has to. I can't live without him."

This was far more information about Karen's marriage than Camille wanted to hear. "I sent Seth to get you some ginger ale. I can't imagine what's keeping him," she said, looking around.

"I'm fine now. I think I'll go home and get some rest before Donald gets home tonight. We have a lot to discuss."

"If you need anything, you know where to find me," Camille told her.

"Thank you. I know we haven't always been friends, but I feel as if you truly mean that."

"I do mean it."

Karen blinked several times and then sighed. "Junior has his car here. Please tell him that he needs to bring Karly home when they're ready to leave."

"I will," Camille promised.

Karen looked as if she had a lot more she wanted to say, but after a moment she simply shrugged and then turned and walked away. Seth touched Camille's arm as she watched Karen disappear into the crowds.

"I have ginger ale," he said, holding out a can that was beaded with sweat.

"Karen decided to go home. You drink it," Camille replied.

He hesitated and then nodded. "I will, actually. I'm still not feeling great."

Max and the children were back before Seth had finished the drink.

"Your mother has gone home," Camille told Junior and Karly. "She wants you to bring Karly home when you're ready to leave," she told Junior.

He made a face. "She's always leaving me stuck with my baby sister."

"I'm not a baby," Karly snapped.

Junior opened his mouth to reply, but Camille cut him off.

"What are you going to ride now?" she asked, looking at Molly and Katie.

"We haven't been on the Super Drop and we haven't been through the Haunted House," Molly told her. "I want to do the mouse again, too."

Max groaned. "I may have to sit out another mouse ride. Let's do the drop thing first though. I think I'll enjoy that one."

He and the four children walked away together, toward the drop ride that towered over the fairgrounds.

"It would take half a million dollars to get me on that thing," Seth told Camille as they watched.

"I'd do that one for pocket change," Camille laughed. "I used to love drop rides, but I'm already feeling a bit queasy and I don't want to push myself today. Maybe I'll try it tomorrow, before the carousel and the Ferris wheel."

"Maybe I'll stay home tomorrow," Seth muttered.

"It's the weekend. Don't you get any days off?"

He shrugged. "I don't have a set schedule. I work when Max needs me and then, when I'm not working, I hang out with Max anyway, because we're friends. It's an odd arrangement, but it seems to work for both of us. I'm not on the clock today, actually. I made sure he was here for his part of the opening ceremony, but now I'm just staying to enjoy the fair."

"You don't seem to be enjoying it very much."

Seth laughed. "It's quite unlike anything I've ever done before. I'm fascinated, really."

"That was awesome," Molly said as she raced back to her mother's side a short time later.

"It was pretty cool," Katie agreed.

"Where are Karly and Junior?" Camille asked as Max came into view.

"Now that their mother is gone, they went to try to find cooler people to hang out with," Molly replied. "If they could have had Max to themselves, they might have stayed with him, but he's being tainted by riding everything with me and Katie."

"Tainted?" Camille repeated.

Molly shrugged. "He's less cool and amazing because he's willing to be seen with me. Is that better?"

"I'm not worried about being cool anymore," Max said with a laugh as he joined them. "I'm too old to be properly cool, although I have to say, I thought that word would have been replaced in modern slang. Is the word cool still relevant?"

Molly laughed. "We have other words that we use, but everyone still uses cool, too."

"Maybe I should learn some of the other words," Max said.

"Old people using teen slang isn't cool," Camille told him. "I work at the school and I hear the slang every day, but I would never use it."

"Some words just aren't mom words," Molly said.

Camille sighed. "You know you're old when. . ."

"So let's go and feel young again," Max suggested. "The haunted house is a walk-through. You don't have to worry about getting dizzy."

"The floors will be uneven and there will be flashing lights and rotating tunnels and all sorts," Camille protested.

"All of that?" Max asked, sounding amused.

"And more," Molly promised him. "Last year they had sliding panels in the floors so that it was almost impossible to get through one of the rooms."

"Fun," Seth said sarcastically.

"I'll do it if you do it," Camille challenged him.

He shrugged. "I think I can handle a haunted house."

"Let's go," Max said brightly.

The haunted house was on its own a short distance from the other rides. The man standing at the door was dressed all in black and he studied them all somberly.

"Are you feeling brave?" he asked in a low voice.

"Yes," Katie giggled.

"Maybe," Molly said.

"This is the most haunted house in the country," they were told. "The owners got so tired of the ghosts and goblins that they sold the house to a stranger over the Internet. They had it raised off its foundations and shipped, just as you see it here, to a family in Maryland. The family moved in right away, but it wasn't long before they began to notice odd things happening."

"Really? Like what?" Seth asked when the man paused.

"Strange noises in the night. Objects moving themselves around the room. They started seeing people in the house, people who weren't meant to be there, people who vanished whenever they were confronted," the man replied.

"So they sold the house to the fair?" Molly asked.

"Oh, no. They simply abandoned it, vowing that they would never take a dime for such a horrible and terrifying object. They left the house and moved to California so that they could be as far away from it as possible."

"So how did it end up here?" Katie demanded.

"Mr. Black, the manager of the fair, let's just say he stumbled across it," the man replied. "He contacted the owners, but they refused to speak to him. Eventually, he got permission from the council in the town in Maryland to take the house away."

Camille looked at Max and raised an eyebrow. That didn't sound strictly legal, but, of course, none of the story was actually true. No doubt the fair's haunted house had been built by a company that manufactured carnival rides, the same as the carousel and the mouse.

"If you're brave enough, you can go inside," the man told them. "I'll need two tickets for each of you, though, as an entry fee. Getting the house here cost Mr. Black a great deal, more than just money, of course."

Molly looked at Max. "Do you think it's worth two tickets?" she asked him.

He shrugged. "We have a lot of tickets left, enough for you to go on the mouse many more times after this."

"Brandon will want to ride a few things," Camille interjected.

Max pulled out the ticket book he'd purchased and flipped through it. "There are at least fifty tickets left in here and I can always buy more," he told Molly.

She exchanged glances with Katie. "It seems kinda lame to me," she said.

The man at the entrance looked shocked. "Lame? My haunted house? I'll tell you what, you give me one ticket each and take your tour. If you aren't terrified out of your wits, or you don't have fun, you don't have to give me the second ticket."

Molly laughed. "That seems a good deal," she said.

Max counted out five tickets and handed them to the man.

"If I were you, I'd send the young ladies in by themselves," the man said as he stepped back to open the door. "Then they can show you just how brave they really are."

Molly and Katie exchanged glances. "We're pretty brave," Molly said. "We'll go first."

The pair disappeared through the door. As the man shut it behind them, Max turned to Camille.

"Are they going to be okay in there?"

"Molly's been coming to the fair since she was a baby. She's been going through the haunted house on her own since she was five. Jason used to dare her to do it. He'd offer her a prize if she managed to get through without crying. She knows it's all make believe and she truly loves pretending to be frightened by it all," Camille assured him.

"What about you?" the man at the door asked in a spooky voice. "How brave are you feeling?"

Camille laughed. "Brave enough for this, anyway."

He winked at her and then stepped back and opened the door.

"Let me go first," Seth said quickly. He took a deep breath and then stepped into the house. "I want to know that there are people behind me to save me when I panic," he called over his shoulder as he plunged into the darkness.

Camille took a cautious step forward and then another. "They've made some changes this year," she said to Max, who was right behind her. She put her hand on the wall to help her find her way. Behind them, the door shut, eliminating what little light they'd had to navigate by.

"I can use the flashlight on my phone," Max offered.

"What fun would that be?" Camille asked. She took another step forward and then gasped as her foot sank into something soft.

"What is it?" Max asked.

"Pillows on the ground," she told him.

It was completely dark, but Camille could sense Max's presence. He was far too close for comfort. Determined to catch up to Seth, she took a few quick steps forward, walking directly into a wall.

"Ouch," she exclaimed.

"Are you okay?" Max asked.

"Fine," she replied quickly. She put her hand in front of her and ran it along the wall. When it reached a corner, she turned ninety degrees, putting up her other hand to feel what was in beside her. Her fingers touched something firm, but softer than a wall. It took her a moment, as her fingers explored, to realize what she'd found.

"Sorry," she muttered, pulling her hand back from Max's chest. *Thank goodness I didn't have my hand any lower*, she thought as she reached for the wall that she knew was in front of her.

"I think the door is here," Max said in her ear. His hand settled into the small of her back and he guided her forward.

"I can manage on my own," she said, taking a large step forward. The ground seemed to give way under her feet and she stumbled.

Max caught her. "Maybe you should slow down," he suggested. "There's no need to rush."

Except being alone in the dark with you is a whole different type of scary, Camille thought. "The kids will be waiting," she said as she took another step forward.

Feeling as if she was inching her way along, Camille felt her way along a short corridor. Near the end, she could see light, which gave her the confidence to walk a bit faster.

Pushing aside heavy cloth strips, the pair found themselves in a large room that was illuminated by flashing lights. Camille blinked several times as her eyes struggled to adapt to the odd lighting. The maze was made up of waist-high bars in a spiral.

"We could duck under," Max suggested.

"Or we could not," she replied. It only took a minute to walk through the spiral to the exit on the opposite side of the room. Max stood and watched her make her way through the maze and then he simply ducked under the bars and crossed to her.

Feeling as if he'd cheated, Camille frowned and then pushed aside the next set of cloth strips. The next room was lit by black lights and she could see panels on the floor that would, no doubt, move when they were walked on.

"Did you want to go first?" she asked Max.

He chuckled. "I will, if you're scared."

"I'm not scared." She took a step forward and then another. As she stepped onto the first panel, it began to slide forward. The one next to it began to slide backwards, making progress almost impossible. The two panels moved back and forth, a few feet in each direction, opposite one another as Camille struggled to walk.

"Walk on the outside edges," Max suggested.

That was the obvious solution, but again, Camille felt as if it was cheating. She grabbed the railing and dragged herself across the room. Max waited until she'd reached the exit before he carefully walked along the panel's edges. It took him only seconds to reach her.

"What's next?" he asked, sounding amused.

Another maze, this time with lights that came on in five-second intervals, gave Max another chance to simply duck under the challenge.

As they left the room, Camille sighed. "You used to do the mazes the way they were designed," she said.

"And then I grew up and learned that if life offers you shortcuts, take them," he replied.

Camille shrugged. "It's a haunted house at the fair. It's not real life. It's meant to be fun."

"Are you having fun?"

"I love spending time with my kids. Watching them have fun is enjoyable for me."

"Molly is lovely. She looks a lot like you did when you were younger."

"She does. Brandon looks more like his father."

They'd reached the end of another short corridor. Camille was fairly certain that the exit was only a few paces ahead, but as they went around a corner, they were plunged into total darkness again.

"It's really good to see you again," Max said in her ear as she stopped to try to work out which way to go.

"Yeah, sure, likewise," she muttered.

He chuckled. "I mean it. I've thought about you a lot over the past thirty years."

"Am I supposed to be flattered?"

"You're supposed to tell me that you thought about me a lot, too, maybe even tell me that you missed me."

Camille swallowed a dozen replies, counting to ten before she spoke. "I don't know what sort of game you're interested in playing, but I'm not taking part," she said, struggling to keep her voice steady.

Max moved beside her and then slid his arms around her. One hand came up and touched her cheek. "There's still a lot of chemistry between us," he whispered.

Camille couldn't argue with the statement. Her heart was

racing and she was feeling a flood of something that could only be described as lust. It had been a long time since she'd felt that particular emotion.

His fingers traced a circle around her lips and then he tipped her chin up to meet his kiss. For Camille, everything vanished around them as she got lost in Max's arms.

"Just like old times," he said huskily when he lifted his head.

"Except I'm not nineteen anymore," she replied. "As pleasant as that was, it isn't an experience I'm interested in repeating. You broke my heart once and that's not something I want to repeat, either."

"Pleasant?" Max echoed, sounding annoyed.

Camille grinned to herself and then pushed him away. Two quick paces down the corridor and another turn around a corner and she could see the outline of the exit door. She pushed her way through the door and then stood, blinking, in the bright sunshine.

CHAPTER 9

"*G*ood for you," Terri said when Camille called her the next morning.

"I was very proud of myself, actually," Camille admitted. "It usually takes me hours to come up with the right reply, but I don't think I could have done better than that one."

"Pleasant?" Terri laughed. "His poor ego must have been shattered."

"If it was, he didn't let it show. He followed me out of the haunted house and then bought us all lunch. By that time, Brandon was done with work, so he joined in the fun and rode everything with Max and Molly and Katie. I spent the afternoon getting to know Seth better."

"Maybe you should date Seth," Terri suggested.

"He's only forty-five and he isn't my type, anyway."

"Maybe I should date Seth."

Camille laughed. "I can fix you up, if you want. He's a bit young for you, but maybe he likes slightly older women."

"Thanks for the *slightly*, but I'm six years older and I'm

not really looking for a man, anyway. Being single agrees with me."

"I'm not looking, either."

"How was the kiss, though?"

Camille blushed. "It was a pretty good kiss," she admitted.

"Pretty good?"

"I felt as if I was nineteen again. If I was the type to jump into bed with a man, I'd have jumped."

Terri laughed. "Okay, then. There's still some chemistry there."

"Way too much. I can't let myself fall for him."

"Maybe he's changed. He did move back to Ramsey, after all."

"Just because he's here at the moment doesn't mean that he's moved back. He's staying at the Riverside and, while he's talking about buying a house, he hasn't actually made an offer anywhere."

"You learned a lot from Seth."

"We had a lot of time to talk. Apparently, Max is mostly here because his mother isn't well, but Max doesn't like to talk about her."

"I heard he's hired several people to look after her so that she isn't ever alone," Terri said.

"Seth wouldn't talk about her at all, but I've heard the same rumors."

"Do you think Max will leave Ramsey once he has his mother's living arrangements sorted out?"

"I can't imagine him staying for long, anyway," Camille sighed.

"I thought you didn't want him around?"

"I don't, not really, but, oh, I don't know. There's a bit of me that still loves him and that bit of me can simply shut up now."

Terri chuckled. "What are you doing today?" she changed

the subject.

"I'm taking the kids back to the fair, of course. Has Thomas been yet?"

"We went last night for the music, but I told him we could go today so he could ride a few rides."

"Want to meet us there? We're going to head there around noon. I don't expect Brandon to be out of bed much before that. I thought we'd get some lunch at the fair and then the kids could ride a few things and we could check out all of the booths before getting more food. We didn't stay for the music last night, but we will tonight, more for the fireworks than for the bands, of course."

"The bands will do their best, but you're right, the fireworks are the best part. We missed the opening show, so I'm really looking forward to tonight."

"Meet us at the barbeque stand at noon," Camille suggested. "That's Brandon's favorite."

"It's Thomas's favorite, too, so that's perfect."

Camille put down the phone and then stretched. She'd rung her friend before she'd even gotten out of bed, eager to share what had happened the previous day with someone. A glance at the clock told her that she still had hours before she needed to get ready to go back to the fair. Sliding back down under the covers, she squeezed her eyes shut and told herself to go back to sleep.

Ten minutes later she was up, starting a load of laundry. Molly joined her in the kitchen a short while later.

"Good morning," she said as she poured herself a glass of milk.

"Good morning," Camille replied. "Why are you up so early?"

"I woke up and I couldn't get back to sleep. I'm excited about going to the fair again today."

"Good. Terri and Thomas are meeting us there."

"Okay."

"It won't be exactly like yesterday, though," Camille warned her. "Today, I'll have to pay for the tickets, so they won't be unlimited."

"Max gave me all of the tickets he had left over after we were done riding yesterday," Molly told her. "I don't think we'll be able to use them all up, even if we try."

Camille frowned. "You should have refused to take them."

"I tried, but he said he was going to be busy today and wouldn't be able to use them himself. He told me that he was just going to throw them away if I didn't take them."

"You should have told me at the time."

"I would have, but you weren't there," Molly replied. "I'm sorry. I didn't mean to upset you."

"It's fine," Camille said, patting her daughter's arm. "You know I don't like you taking gifts from anyone, aside from family or close friends."

"But we'd spent the whole day with him. I thought he was your friend."

"It's complicated."

"He seemed really nice. You let him buy us all lunch, too," Molly pointed out.

"Like I said, it's complicated," Camille sighed. "Let's talk about something else."

"Do you think you could fall in love with him again?"

"That isn't something else."

"No, but he seems nice and he's very, very rich, isn't he?"

"I'm quite happy on my own."

"But think how nice it would be to have all that lovely money at our disposal."

"It doesn't necessarily work that way. Anyway, whatever I think of him, he has to want to get married and settle in Ramsey and I can't see Max Steward doing either of those things."

"He said he was really happy to be back in Ramsey."

"For now," Camille said. "There's no reason to believe he's going to stay long-term."

"Maybe we could…"

Camille held up a hand, stopping Molly mid-sentence. "Max isn't looking for a wife or an instant family, which is what he would get with me. He and I were friends many years ago and it was fun spending some time with him yesterday, but that was as far as it goes. I don't expect to see him again and I don't particularly want to see him again, either."

That last part might not have been strictly true, but Camille wanted to do what she could to stop her daughter from imagining a wonderful new life funded by Max's generosity. That wasn't going to happen and the sooner Molly accepted it, the better.

Terri and Thomas were waiting when Camille and the children arrived at the fair just before noon.

"Food first, then rides, then ice cream and cotton candy," Molly suggested.

"Definitely food first," Camille agreed. "I don't know about ice cream and cotton candy, though."

"We have ride tickets for everyone," Molly told Terri and Thomas. "Max bought zillions of them yesterday and gave me the extra."

Camille patted her purse. "We have a lot more than we'll need, so don't buy any," she said.

Terri grinned. "In that case, I'll treat everyone to ice cream after a few rides."

"Yes," Brandon and Thomas exclaimed together.

The women sent the kids to find a picnic table in the shade while they joined the end of the line at the barbeque stand.

"I'm surprised you let Molly take the extra tickets," Terri

said as the children walked away.

"She didn't mention it to me until this morning," Camille replied.

"That was clever of her."

Camille laughed. "I suppose it was, really. I wouldn't have let her take them if I'd known. She told me that Max said he was simply going to throw them away if she didn't take them, though."

"I suppose he can afford to throw away money."

They ordered enough food for a small army and then carried full trays away from the counter. The boys jumped up to help as Camille and Terri reached the table area.

"Thank you for helping," Camille said once they were all seated. "I'm sure it was more starvation than a desire to be helpful that prompted it, but I won't complain."

Brandon laughed. "I didn't get breakfast," he reminded her around a mouthful of lunch.

"You only got out of bed half an hour ago," Molly said. "This is your breakfast."

"Lucky," Thomas said. "My mom made me get up at eight to do homework."

"I did my summer homework in June," Brandon replied. "I knew I was going to be working all summer and I didn't want to have to do it all during the last week before school starts again."

Thomas made a face. "I started it this morning."

Molly laughed. "We don't have summer homework in middle school," she said happily.

"But you'll be in high school one day and then you'll have tons of it," Thomas told her. "I shouldn't have taken so many AP classes."

"You're taking two," Brandon said. "I'm taking four."

"Yeah, but you're smarter than I am," Thomas shot back.

Brandon laughed. "I'm smart enough to have my summer

homework done, anyway."

After lunch, the kids went on the rides while Terri and Camille watched.

"I wish Katie was here again," Molly complained after a short while. "Most of the rides are for two people and the boys always want to go together. I keep ending up alone or having to sit with a stranger."

"I'll ride a few things with you," Terri offered. "Nothing too crazy, though."

When they got tired of rides, Terri bought everyone ice cream and then they wandered through the booths, chatting to the people they knew, who seemed to be everywhere.

"It's nearly dinner time," Thomas said around five o'clock.

"We had a huge lunch and ice cream after that," Terri replied. "Surely you can't be hungry."

"I'm starving," he told her. "I think I could eat an entire pizza right now."

"Convenient that we happen to be standing in front of the pizza stand, isn't it?" Terri said dryly.

Thomas shrugged. "It doesn't have to be pizza, really. I'll eat anything."

"Don't I know it," Terri laughed. "How does pizza sound to everyone else?"

No one objected, so Terri and Camille bought three large pizzas and cans of soda for everyone. There was another cluster of picnic tables near the pizza stand, so they sat together and dug in.

"It's good to sit down," Camille said as she picked out a slice of pizza.

"At least I got to sit down for a few minutes on each ride," Terri laughed. "I got to be spun around and made dizzy, too."

"Lucky you," Camille replied.

"Cotton candy for dessert?" Molly asked.

Remembering the last time she'd had cotton candy,

Camille flushed. "Maybe we can find something else to have for dessert," she suggested. "Something that isn't pure sugar."

There were several booths holding bake sales and as it was the last day of the fair, everything was being discounted. Molly got a chocolate cupcake with chocolate icing. Thomas and Brandon both got brownies. Camille selected a chocolate chip cookie.

"Nothing for me," Terri said. "I may be riding a few more rides and I'm afraid I ate too much pizza."

After another walk around the entire fairgrounds, Terri let the kids drag her back on the rides. Camille found a bench under a tree and sat down to people watch.

"Hello, Camille," a friendly voice said a short while later.

Camille, who had been watching a young mother trying to convince her toddler that it was time to leave, turned and smiled at Jana Bailey.

Jana was a few years younger than Camille and had only been living in Ramsey for around five years. Camille didn't know her well, but Jana's son, Shawn, took Tae Kwon Do with her kids.

"Hello, Jana. Are you having fun at the fair?" Camille replied.

"It's always fun. It's one of the things I like best about living in Ramsey, actually. Not just the fair, but all of the special events that bring the town together. When Simon died, I thought about moving back to Pennsylvania or even somewhere further afield, but Shawn and I had both already fallen under Ramsey's spell."

Camille nodded. "I've been here my whole life and I can't imagine living anywhere else."

"Mom loved it here, too," Jana added. "I hope Shawn will decide to go to the college here. Because I work there, he can go for free."

"Maybe I need to apply for a job at the college," Camille

said.

Jana shook her head. "Openings don't come up very often and I've been hearing rumors of cutbacks, as well. You might be better off staying where you are."

"Luckily, I love my job. I wish it came with free college tuition for my kids, though."

"You get summers off, though. I've been working all summer trying to get all of the professors in my department ready for September."

"If professors are anything like teachers, that will have been hard work."

"It is definitely that," Jana laughed.

"Is Shawn riding the rides?"

"Yes, he met up with some school friends to go on a few rides. Someone had a stack of tickets from somewhere, which was a nice surprise for me. Ride tickets seem to get more and more expensive every year."

"Everything gets more expensive every year," Camille replied. "At the fair, at the grocery store, everywhere."

Jana nodded. "My department is hoping for a donation from Maxwell Steward. I don't suppose you know anything about his plans?"

Camille flushed. "Nothing at all. We've barely spoken since he's been back and before that I hadn't seen him in over thirty years."

"Someone told me that you and he spent the day at the fair together yesterday," Jana told her. "The whole town is dying to know if he's just visiting or if he's actually moving back to Ramsey."

"You'd have to ask him. I don't much care either way."

Jana looked surprised. "He could do a lot of good for the town, though."

"He could, but I suspect he'll only be interested in projects that are also good for him."

Before Jana could reply, Molly came running up. Camille could see the others following more slowly behind her.

"It's almost time for the fireworks," Molly said. "We have to get our special spot."

Camille nodded and got to her feet. "It was nice talking to you," she said to Jana, who was also standing up.

"I'm sure I'll see you at Tae Kwon Do," Jana replied. "We're always there."

"Us, too," Camille laughed.

"Where are we going?" Terri asked as Camille began to walk away from the rides.

"We always watch the fireworks from the corner of the fairgrounds," Molly told her. "There's a special spot, but you'll see."

Five minutes later, Camille stopped and frowned. "Or maybe not," she said in a low voice.

"They can't block off our special spot," Molly nearly shouted.

The quiet corner of the fairgrounds, which had an uninterrupted view of the entire site, was now fenced off. A small tent had been set up in one corner of the enclosed area. There was a man in a security uniform guarding the entrance.

"This wasn't here a few hours ago," Camille said to him.

"It's VIP viewing for the fireworks," he explained. "They get wine and beer and snacks in the tent and then they get the best possible view of the fireworks."

"I didn't think anyone else knew this was the best place for viewing the fireworks," Camille replied.

He chuckled. "Everyone wants to be in front of the stage, but that's really too close to properly appreciate the show. The smart people always came and stood back here to watch."

"People like me, and now we can't," Camille sighed.

"You're welcome on the other side of the fence," he told them.

"It won't be the same," Molly said. "We've been watching the fireworks from the top of the slope for my entire life." She gestured toward the gentle slope within the enclosed area.

"I'm sorry," the guard said, sounding genuinely apologetic. "We've more VIPs than ever before this year and the organizers wanted to do something special for them."

"It's fine," Camille lied. "Come on guys. Let's find another spot."

"Hello, hello," Karen Henderson-Archer said, waving at Camille and the others. "Isn't this just the best thing ever?" She waved a card at the security guard and then sailed into the VIP area. Her husband and their children followed behind her.

"How come they get in?" Molly demanded.

"Dr. Archer is a generous supporter of the fair," the guard told her.

Camille sighed. "Come on," she said firmly. "We'll find a better spot somewhere."

They'd only walked a few steps away when Camille heard her name.

"Camille?"

She turned around and frowned at Max, who was looking out from behind the security fence. "Hello," she said brightly. "We're just off to find a spot for viewing the fireworks."

"You should join me in here," he suggested. "Everyone knows this is the best place for viewing them."

"Can we?" Molly asked quickly.

"I'm sure Max can't get all of us in," Camille countered. "There are too many of us."

"How many?" Max asked.

"Five," Molly replied.

Camille could see that her daughter was holding her breath as she waited to hear what Max would say next.

"I can get you all in," he assured her.

"I don't think…" Camille began.

"Please," Max interrupted. "It's unbelievably dull in here. Nearly everyone is either old or arrogant or both. Come and keep me company."

Before Camille could argue any further, Terri grabbed her arm. "Let's go," she said. "I want to be a VIP."

Feeling as if she'd been overruled, Camille followed the others through the gate, smiling at the security guard who looked happy for them.

Half an hour later, a cold drink in her hand, she stood between her children on the slightly raised grass and waited for the fireworks to begin.

"He's really nice," Terri hissed in Camille's ear as she wiggled her way into a spot in front of her.

"I'm sure," Camille replied.

"You should have come and talked with us. We had great fun," Terri told her.

"I was busy with the children," Camille said. *Busy making them talk to me so that I didn't have to talk to Max*, she added to herself.

"Whatever," Terri said, shaking her head.

"Ladies and gentlemen, please be certain that you are happy with your location. We will be turning off the lights in the enclosure in five seconds," a voice announced.

Molly squealed and then squeezed her mother's hand. "This is even better than last year," she said happily.

Just before the lights went off, Camille noticed Max. He was standing on the edge of the crowd and when their eyes met, he smiled and began to move toward her. The entire fairgrounds were plunged into darkness as he reached her side.

CHAPTER 10

"This was always our spot," Max said in Camille's ear.

"It was our spot for a few years and then Jason and I used to come here to watch the fireworks," she replied. "I've been bringing the children here since they were babies."

"I understand Jason is coming for a visit," Max said.

"Is he? I didn't know."

"He told me he was staying with you."

"And I told him that he wasn't welcome in my house," Camille said angrily.

"We'll sort it out later. For now, watch the fireworks," Max told her.

Camille opened her mouth to object and then shut it again as the first rocket shot into the air. For fifteen minutes, the skies were illuminated by some of the most beautiful fireworks Camille had ever seen. Or maybe it just felt that way with Max standing right behind her, his hand idly moving up and down her back. Maybe she was the only one seeing fireworks, she thought as what seemed like a thousand rockets exploded all at once above them.

The crowd cheered loudly and then, without warning, the lights around the enclosure came back on. Camille jumped away from Max, blinking as her eyes tried to adjust to the sudden change.

"The entire committee at Ramsey Fair Days wants to thank Maxwell Steward for providing tonight's amazing fireworks extravaganza," the announcement over the loud-speakers said. "Thank you, Max, and welcome home."

The people in the VIP area gave Max a short round of applause. Camille found herself walking backward slowly, putting distance between herself and the man who still made her heart beat faster, in spite of everything that had happened between them.

"Mom? What now?" Molly demanded.

"Now we go home and get some sleep," Camille replied. "It's Monday tomorrow. Brandon has to work and you have training tomorrow night. I have to work, as well, but only for half of the day."

"Which half?" Molly wanted to know.

"I have to take Brandon to work at seven, so I may as well just go to work from there," she replied. "I'll be home around one, assuming everything goes to plan."

"We could have done my back to school shopping tomorrow," Molly grumbled.

"But now it's done. Maybe we can do something fun tomorrow."

"Like what?"

"Do you want to go to the zoo?" Camille asked, knowing what the answer would be.

"Can we? I love the zoo," Molly said excitedly. "Can I invite Katie to come along?"

"Sure, why not? If she can come, have her meet us at our house at two. We'll go to the zoo and then she's welcome to stay for dinner. I'll make spaghetti."

"Yay!" Molly shouted. "It will be an almost perfect day."

"Someone is happy," Max remarked as he walked up behind them.

Camille jumped and then sighed. "We're just making plans for tomorrow," she explained. "But now we need to go."

"What are you going to be doing tomorrow, then?" Max asked.

"I have to work," Camille snapped. "And that means I need sleep."

She grabbed Molly's arm and quickly walked away from the man, calling to Brandon as she went. Terri and Thomas ran after them.

"Are you okay?" Terri asked when they reached the parking lot.

"I'm just tired of seeing Max Steward everywhere I go. I'll be happier when he goes back to the city," Camille replied.

"What if he doesn't go back?" Terri asked. "He said he's planning to stay for a while, anyway."

"He'll go back sooner or later. There's nothing to keep him here, not really."

"His mother is here," Terri reminded her.

"But he can afford to move her anywhere." She sighed. "I don't want to talk about Max anymore."

"Okay, I'll see you at the school tomorrow," Terri said. She gave her a hug before she and Thomas walked away.

"Mom, are you okay?" Brandon asked.

"I'm fine. I'm just tired," Camille replied as they got into the car.

She was tired, but that didn't mean that she could sleep once she got into bed. Her back felt itchy all along the path that Max had traced during the fireworks. In the small bathroom that was attached to the master bedroom, she opened the medicine cabinet. Her doctor had given her sleeping pills when Jason had first left and she'd found sleeping difficult.

After taking them for a few nights, she'd decided that she had hated the drowsy feeling they'd left her with the next day. Now she wasn't so sure. She really wanted to stop thinking about Max and the pills would make sure she did just that.

The bottle was on the bottom shelf and it was covered in a fine layer of dust. According to the label, the pills had expired four years earlier. That would probably mean that they'd be less potent, she thought as she struggled with the childproof cap. Sighing, she threw the unopened bottle into the garbage can and crawled back into bed. After counting three thousand, four hundred, and sixty-three sheep, she fell into a restless slumber.

* * *

DRAGGING herself out of bed the next morning wasn't easy and she found herself shouting at Brandon as the seconds ticked away and it began to look as if he was going to be late for work.

"Mom, are you okay?" Molly asked as Camille stood at the bottom of the stairs and shouted to Brandon for what felt like the millionth time.

Camille took a deep breath. "I didn't sleep well. I'm tired and your brother is going to be late for work, which means I'll end up late for work, too."

"I'll go and talk to him," she said. "You go and have another cup of coffee."

Feeling like the worst mother in the world, Camille went back to the kitchen and poured herself another cup of coffee. As the caffeine began to work its magic, she could hear Molly talking to Brandon.

"...now before Mom loses her mind."

"I'm up," Brandon muttered.

Ten minutes later he thundered down the stairs, his hair

still wet from what had to have been the shortest shower he'd ever taken. Molly followed him into the kitchen with a satisfied look on her face.

"Thank you," Camille told her daughter. "I'll be back before one, assuming nothing disastrous happens. Mrs. Blake should be here in another hour or so."

Molly made a face. "I don't need a babysitter," she complained.

"Mrs. Blake isn't a babysitter. She's just coming over to keep you company until I get home. If I thought you needed a babysitter, I'd have someone here now."

"Whatever," Molly said grumpily.

Camille swallowed the last of her coffee and then rushed Brandon out to the car. "I'll pick you up at six," she told him as she pulled up in front of the Tae Kwon Do school. "Have fun."

"We're taking the kids to the park today," he told her. "It's unbelievably hard work."

"Remember that when you start thinking about having children," Camille told him with a laugh.

"At least I'll only have one at a time," he remarked.

"Not necessarily," she replied.

The school was still locked when she arrived. She rang the security office and asked to be let in.

"We weren't expecting anyone this early," the female security guard told her as she opened the front door.

"I can get my work done at any time and Brandon had to work at seven, so it made sense to just come in and get what needs doing done."

"Have a nice day," the guard told her as Camille unlocked her office.

She looked at the pile of papers on her desk and sighed. Getting out by one was going to be a struggle. Two hours later, she looked up from the pile of student schedules that she was sorting and sighed. What had Jana said about jobs at the college, she thought. The phone startled her.

"Camille? It's Mrs. Blake. How you live your life is your business, of course, but I wanted to make sure that what I was being told was correct."

Camille frowned at the phone. "I'm sorry, but what?"

"He says he's your ex-husband and that you told him he could stay in your spare room. To my mind, that isn't where ex-husbands belong, but Molly seems happy to see him."

"Jason is there," Camille said flatly.

"He is, with several suitcases," Mrs. Blake confirmed.

"He isn't staying in my spare room," Camille told her. "I don't care what he says. I told him he wasn't welcome. This isn't your problem, though. I'll come home and deal with it."

"Now don't you worry about that," Mrs. Blake replied. "If you say he isn't welcome, I'll pass that along. If he gives me any grief, I'll call Stanley and let him sort it out."

Camille grinned. As much as Molly didn't care for the woman, there were a number of reasons why Camille was always happy to leave Mrs. Blake in charge of her children. The woman was nearly seventy, but she'd raised four boys on her own after her husband had passed away suddenly. She was still as strong and independent as she'd been when she'd been left on her own at twenty-seven with four children under the age of six. Her youngest, Stanley, was a policeman with the Ramsey police force and Camille had no doubt that he'd drop whatever he was doing and rush to help his mother if she called him to complain about Jason.

"I'll be home as soon as I can be," Camille promised.

"Don't you worry about us. We'll be fine," Mrs. Blake replied.

Camille put the phone down and then sighed. Jason would be furious with her when Mrs. Blake told him he couldn't stay. She just had to hope that Molly and Brandon would understand why she'd told their father to leave, especially since it had been such a long time since they'd seen him.

It took her another half hour to finish sorting the schedules. Once that was done, she grabbed a pile of papers that needed typing and tucked them into her bag. She'd take them home and work on them after the kids were in bed, she decided. The school had a few laptops that could be borrowed for such occasions. She added one to her bag and then shut down her desktop machine. Switching the phones back to the answering machine, she switched off the lights and headed for the door.

An unfamiliar car was parked on her driveway when she got home a short while later.

"Hello?" she called as she opened the door.

"Camille?" Jason's voice made her frown.

She stopped in the doorway and braced herself for the inevitable flood of emotions that would accompany seeing him again.

"What's this about me not being allowed to stay?" the man demanded as he stormed out of the living room and into the foyer.

"Now, now, Mr. Quinn," Mrs. Blake said from behind him. "I told you what Miss Camille said. Don't you dare try to bully her into changing her mind."

"I'm not bullying anyone," Jason said through gritted teeth.

"I'm sorry, Jason," Camille said, "but the spare room is now the kids' playroom and I'm not making them clear away their things for you. You can get a room at a hotel somewhere."

"I can clear up the spare room," Molly offered as she came into view.

Jason gave Camille a smug smile. "My daughter wants me to stay," he said.

"It isn't her decision. Even if the spare room was ready for guests, which it isn't, you aren't staying here," Camille said firmly. "You chose to move out five years ago. You can't simply move back in on another whim."

"Wanting to see my children isn't a whim," Jason protested.

"And I'm happy to let you spend some time with them, but it won't be here. This is my home, and theirs. It's not yours. Let me know when you've found a place to stay and then we can discuss the children's schedules. Brandon is working quite a bit, though. He may not have a lot of time to spend with you," Camille told him.

"Molly and I are going to the zoo this afternoon," Jason told her.

Camille looked at her daughter and frowned. "Are you?"

Molly flushed. "I thought maybe we could all go," she muttered.

Counting to ten as she took a deep breath, Camille exhaled slowly. "I'm sorry, Molly, but I'd rather not spend the afternoon with your father. If you want to go to the zoo with him, you can, though."

"Oh, come on," Jason said. "Surely you can endure a few hours at the zoo with me for the sake of Molly's happiness. She wants us all to go together. You want to make her happy, don't you?"

Camille turned and stared at him for a minute. "I've spent the last five years doing everything in my power to make her and her brother happy. I'm the one who's been there when they've sobbed their eyes out trying to understand how their father could have simply walked out on them. I'm the one who's paid all of the bills and done without so that they can have the things they need. I'm the one who's assured them, over and over again, that their father still loves them, even though he never calls and never bothers to come and see them. Don't you dare question what I'm prepared to do to make my children happy."

He shrugged. "I've been busy. I never meant to leave it so long, but, well, that's all water under the bridge. I'm here now."

"Great. Go and get yourself a room somewhere and then you can take Molly to the zoo later," Camille told him.

"I think I'd rather go with you," Molly said to Camille.

"Oh, terrific," Jason snapped. "Now you're making our daughter, our eleven-year-old daughter, choose between us. I hope you're proud of yourself."

"She's twelve," Camille said icily. "If you sent her cards for her birthday, you might be better able to remember her age."

"I send cards," he protested. "Sometimes."

"Sometimes, even though she has a birthday every single year," Camille snapped. "I want you to leave now and I don't want to see you again. We can arrange visits with the children by phone and I'll make sure they have rides for those visits. That's all I'm prepared to do for you."

"I understand you've been spending a lot of time with Max Steward," Jason sneered. "He broke your heart, too. I suppose you're more willing to forgive him because he's rich and I'm not."

"I haven't forgiven him for anything but at least he only broke my heart. Your behavior has crushed our children's hearts and that's what I can't forgive," she replied.

"Molly doesn't seem crushed. She was really happy to see me."

"Because I want it all to be okay again," Molly said through tears. "I want you to come back and be my dad again. I want to wake up on Sunday mornings and find you making pancakes for everyone. I want everything to be the way it was before you left."

Jason looked surprised. "I don't know that we can go back to how it was before, but I do miss you and Brandon. As your mother doesn't want me staying here, though, things won't quite be the way they were before."

"Let's take things one step at a time," Camille said, working to keep her voice steady. "Molly, I think you should go to the zoo with your father this afternoon. I'm sure you'll have fun."

"Katie is supposed to be coming, too," Molly said.

Jason made a face. "I don't know…" he said slowly.

"Already he's making excuses," Mrs. Blake interjected.

Flushing, Jason shook his head. "I just want some time with my daughter, just the two of us, that's all."

"Come back at one o'clock," Camille told him. "I'll sort things out with Katie's mother."

"Great. I'll see you later, peanut," Jason said as he headed for the door.

Molly sighed. "No one calls me peanut anymore," she told him.

He shrugged. "I'll try to remember."

As he shut the door behind himself, Camille sank down onto the small cedar chest near the door. It was convenient for putting on and taking off shoes, but now it was the only thing that kept her from falling to the ground.

"Are you okay?" Molly asked as tears began to flow down Camille's cheeks.

She sighed and then nodded. "I'm okay, really. Seeing your father again was just something of a shock, that's all."

"He seemed like a stranger," Molly said sadly.

"I'm sorry I can't let him stay here."

"I don't really want him here. Sharing a bathroom with Brandon is bad enough."

Camille chuckled through her tears. "I love you, baby girl."

She wiped her eyes and then she called Katie's mother and explained about the change to the zoo trip before she and Molly and Mrs. Blake had lunch together.

CHAPTER 11

"Where is he?" Molly demanded at quarter past one.

"I've no idea," Camille said with a sigh. She never should have agreed to let Molly go anywhere with the man, she thought to herself. He was completely unreliable now.

"Maybe we should just go to the zoo," Molly suggested. "Leave him a note. He can meet us there if he ever shows up here."

Camille shook her head. "He's probably just running a bit late. He's never been good at being on time." Her words were true and as she said them Camille thought she should have seen his behavior during their marriage as a warning of what was to come.

She'd always been the one who'd kept track of where they were supposed to be and when. He'd been late for their wedding and he'd very nearly missed Brandon's birth. Even before he'd decided to run away from his responsibilities, she'd not been able to completely rely on him. He would regularly change jobs almost on a whim. He'd treated himself to an expensive watch with one of his bonuses, even though the house had needed a new roof.

Looking back, Camille could list over a dozen times when he'd let her down during the years of their marriage, but that hadn't meant that she hadn't been completely blindsided when he'd left her. She'd been just as shocked when he'd had his affair, but that wasn't something she was going to let herself think about, and it wasn't anything the children needed to know about, either.

"There he is," Molly said a few minutes later. She had the front door open before Camille could reply.

"Let's go see the animals," Jason said when he reached Molly. "Are you sure you don't want to come?" he asked Camille.

"I have work to do," Camille replied. "Someone has to pay the bills."

Jason frowned. "I'm going to start looking for a job soon," he told her. "Then I'll be able to help more. I know Brandon wants to move to the city for college. I plan to do everything I can to help him with that."

"I think he'd be better off staying here and studying at Hailwood like I did," Camille replied.

"Hailwood? I mean, it's an okay school, but he'll learn a lot more about the world in the city," Jason countered.

"Let's not have this conversation right now," Camille said. "Molly needs to be home by five so she can have dinner before training tonight."

"Training?"

"I'm testing for my black belt in Tae Kwon Do in December," Molly said proudly. "I've been training for almost three years now."

"So it won't hurt if you miss a class or two," Jason suggested. "We haven't seen each other in five years."

"But training is important," Molly told him. "You can come and watch, if you want."

"We'll see how the day goes," Jason said.

Molly gave her mother a hug and then followed Jason out the door. Camille shut the door with tears in her eyes. Molly was so happy to see her father that she seemed willing to forgive and forget about the past five years. Brandon was unlikely to be as forgiving, but regardless, Camille was worried that Jason's return would be short lived and that the children would be left broken-hearted yet again.

She set up the laptop and forced herself to work for several hours. Her typing was riddled with errors, but she kept at it, not letting herself think about what might be happening at the zoo. By five-thirty, though, she was starting to worry. It was almost time to go and get Brandon when Jason finally pulled into the driveway.

Molly jumped out of the car and ran through the door. "I don't have time to eat," she shouted as she headed for the stairs. "I want to take class at six."

"You have to eat or you won't have enough energy for class," Camille called after her.

"Give her a break. She had popcorn at the zoo," Jason said from the doorway.

Camille spun around. "Popcorn isn't going to get her through a twenty minute warm up and forty minutes of Tae Kwon Do," she snapped.

"She's young. She'll be fine."

Counting to ten, Camille forced herself to take a deep breath before she replied. "You've no idea…" she began.

A loud buzzing noise interrupted her. Jason pulled out an expensive cell phone and glanced at the screen.

"Gotta take this," he said, turning his back on Camille.

She went into the kitchen and put together a snack for Molly. A peanut butter sandwich and a banana would be just enough to keep her going through her class, Camille thought. She added a square of chocolate to the bag and then returned to the foyer. Jason was just dropping his phone into his pocket as Molly thundered down the stairs in her uniform.

"You look great," Jason told her. "It reminds me of when Brandon first started, like ten years ago."

"Thanks," Molly said, blushing. "Wait until you see what I can do."

He sighed. "Yeah, sorry, but I'm not going to be able to come to your class after all. An old friend just called and wants to see me tonight. I couldn't refuse, really. I'll come to another practice, another time, okay?"

Camille watched her daughter's face fall. "Another time?" Molly repeated.

"You train like five times a week," Jason laughed. "You told me that yourself. I can watch you any night. I need to see this guy tonight."

Molly nodded. "Sure, whatever, have fun."

"I don't know if it will be fun, but it may lead to a job down the road," Jason said. "That's important for all of us."

"Good luck," Molly said.

Camille was silent as Jason smiled and waved before he headed back to his car.

"He said he couldn't wait to see me doing Tae Kwon Do," Molly said through tears.

"He's right, though. He needs a job," Camille replied. "Why don't you have something to eat and then take the late class? I'll go and get Brandon for now."

Molly took a deep breath and then slowly shook her head. "I know you've put a snack together for me, haven't you?"

"Of course."

"Then let's go," she said tightly. "I won't let that man keep me from doing what I want to do."

"Good girl," Camille replied, so angry at Jason that she could barely speak.

Molly ate everything in the bag on the short drive. "I'm okay," she told Camille as they got out of the car. "I wonder if Brandon will even get to see Dad. Now that he's reconnected with some old friends, he'll probably be too busy for us."

"I'm sorry I didn't let him stay with us," Camille said, feeling guilty.

"I'm not. He should have to make some effort to see us. That's how we'll know if he really cares or not."

"He cares, he's just, well, he's a bit selfish, that's all."

"More than a bit," Molly said quietly. They walked into the building together and then Molly disappeared into the locker room. Camille said hello to Master Caldwell who was behind the desk by the door and then she found a seat in the small foyer. Brandon found her there a few minutes later.

"I'm done and I'm too tired to take class," he told her as he dropped onto the couch next to her.

"You're sunburned, too," she replied, studying his red face and even redder ears.

"I made them all put on sunscreen before we went to the park," Muriel Kane, the school's administrator, called from where she'd joined Master Caldwell behind the desk.

"I didn't use enough," Brandon said.

"Clearly," Camille said with a smile. "We have lotion for sunburn at home. Make sure you use a lot of it when we get home."

Brandon nodded. "Molly told me that Dad's in town," he said after a moment.

"He is. I'm not letting him stay with us, though," Camille replied.

"That's good. I don't want to see him."

"He's in favor of you going to the city for college."

"I don't want or need his support," Brandon snapped.

Camille raised an eyebrow. Brandon sighed. "Okay, I do need his support if I'm going to move to the city, but he isn't really going to help me. He's going to say all the right things and then let me down in the end, the same as always."

"Let's not worry about all of that for tonight. Do you really not want to see him while he's here?"

"I don't know. Molly said he took her to the zoo and then wouldn't listen when she said she needed to get home. Then, when he was supposed to come and watch her tonight, he decided to go out with some friends instead."

"I believe that's right," Camille said, swallowing a sigh.

"So why would I want to see him?"

"Because he's your father and he loves you, even if he is being rather selfish at the moment," Camille suggested.

Brandon shook his head. "I don't understand him."

"I don't either, but you have a chance now to ask him to explain himself."

"That might be worth seeing him for, actually. I'd love to see him try to explain why he left us."

So would I, Camille thought. She'd asked Jason to explain hundreds of times and she'd yet to get an answer that made sense to her.

"I have the day off tomorrow. Maybe I should call him and see if he wants to do something," Brandon said thoughtfully.

"You could try. He may not answer, if he's out with friends."

Brandon nodded and then pulled out his cell phone. He scrolled through his contact list and then tapped on an old picture of Jason. Winking at his mother, he put the call on speakerphone.

"Dad? It's Brandon," he said when they heard a muffled hello.

"Brandon? Hey, hi. Hey, can I call you back? It's really noisy here. I'll call you tomorrow, okay?"

"Yeah, sure," Brandon muttered.

"Next round is on Max," Jason shouted just before he ended the call.

"So he's with Max," Brandon said as he put his phone away. "I suppose I can see why he'd rather be with Max than me and Molly."

"He said he's trying to find a job. Max could be a valuable asset to his job hunt."

"He had a job. He had a good job before he decided that he didn't want to be an adult anymore," Brandon said, his voice rising.

Camille put a hand on his arm. "I know you're mad and you have every right to be, but this isn't the place for this conversation."

"I'm okay," Brandon told her. "For what it's worth, I'm back to not wanting to see him."

"We'll worry about that when he calls you tomorrow."

"I think you mean *if* he calls me tomorrow," Brandon replied darkly.

"Let's get ice cream," Camille suggested once Molly was finished with her class.

"Oh, yes, please," Molly said happily.

It only took them a few minutes to get to Bessie's. As Camille pulled into the parking lot, Brandon made a noise.

"What's wrong?" Camille asked.

"Max is here," he said.

"We don't have to stop," Camille offered.

"Oh, no, I don't mind seeing Max," Brandon explained. "I'm just wondering who was with Dad when I spoke to him."

"Let's not worry about your father for tonight," Camille said. "Let's get triple scoops with extra hot fudge."

"Yay!" Molly cheered.

As they walked to the counter, Molly waved to Max who was sitting with Seth at one of the tables. He waved back and then walked over to join them.

"Triple scoops with extra hot fudge for everyone," Camille told Janet. The children chose their flavors which gave Camille time to decide what she wanted. After Janet passed over the huge bowls of ice cream, Max handed the woman the money to pay for them.

"I'll pay for my own ice cream," Camille snapped.

Max shook his head. "You've had a bad day. Jason is back in town. The least a friend can do is buy you some ice cream."

"We aren't friends," she told him crossly.

"We could be, if you'd stop being so hostile toward me," he countered.

Molly began to giggle and Brandon sighed. "Just let him pay for the ice cream," he suggested. "We're holding up the line."

Camille looked behind them at the young couple that was waiting to order. "Sorry," she muttered, picking up her bowl and walking away.

"Max, your change," Janet called after them.

"Keep it," Max replied, keeping pace with Camille as she made her way toward the picnic tables.

"Can I go and sit with Jen?" Molly asked, waving to one of her school friends who was sitting several tables away.

"Sure," Camille replied.

"Dave's here," Brandon said. "I haven't seen him all summer."

"So go," Camille sighed.

"They don't want to sit with us in case we argue more," Max suggested as he sat down next to Camille opposite Seth.

"I'm going to go and make that phone call," Seth said, getting to his feet and walking quickly away.

"We aren't going to argue. We aren't even going to speak," she told Max. She took a large bite of ice cream and let it melt in her mouth.

"How did you know Jason was in town?" she asked before her next bite.

He chuckled. "Not speaking didn't last long, then," he teased. "Jason called me. I'm putting him up in a room at the Riverside. I haven't seen him yet, but we're supposed to have lunch together tomorrow."

"When Brandon talked to him earlier, Jason said something to someone he called Max," Camille replied, aware that her tone made her words sound like an accusation.

Max shrugged. "Believe it or not, I'm not the only man in the world named Max. It's entirely possible that there's another man in Ramsey with that name, even. I don't know how likely it is that that man was with Jason tonight, but stranger things have happened."

"Or Jason wanted the kids to think he was hanging out with you as an excuse for not spending time with them," Camille sighed.

"Jason and I weren't close friends in school, but he was an okay guy. I can't believe he's treating you and his children so badly."

"He had a fairly rough childhood with parents who had very high expectations for him. He worked incredibly hard to make them proud, but neither of them ever seemed at all impressed with what he accomplished. They both passed away about a year before my father died. I told you before that my father's death made him completely reevaluate his life."

Max nodded. "Are you okay?" he asked softly.

Camille thought for a moment and then nodded. "I was worried that I might still have feelings for him, that seeing him again might be difficult, but it wasn't like that at all. I feel sorry for the children, because they crave his love and approval, and I feel sorry for him because he's missing out on being a part of the lives of two amazing kids, but aside from that, I'm doing okay."

"You must be angry with him."

"Some, not so much for what he did in the past as for what he's doing now. He took Molly to the zoo and then brought her back late and dumped her even though he'd said he'd come and watch her train. She doesn't understand why her father would do that to her."

"I don't either," Max replied.

Camille shrugged. "After his parents died, our marriage started to fall apart. I did my best to hide what was happening from the children. Maybe that was a mistake. When Jason left, it was much more of a shock for them than it was for me."

"Your ice cream is melting," Max told her.

She ate the rest of her sweet treat while staring straight ahead, trying to gather her thoughts. As she scraped up the last few bites of hot fudge, Max spoke again.

"Have dinner with me tomorrow night," he suggested. "Let's get to know one another again."

"Thank you, but no," she replied firmly. "I'm doing okay on my own and I don't need another broken heart, not after all these years. Our lives have taken very different paths. You aren't going to be happy staying in Ramsey, not for long, not after everything else you've done. I can't imagine leaving Ramsey. Besides, you broke my heart first, before Jason had a chance to shatter it again. I'm better off without either of you in my life."

Max stared at her for a moment. "Don't compare me to Jason," he said eventually. "I was twenty-two and ambitious. I was impatient and didn't want to wait for you to finish school before I started making my fortune. If I had it to do over again, I'd do things differently, but whatever, I didn't mean to hurt you. I simply couldn't see past my own ambition. Don't try to equate that with a man in his forties leaving his wife and children because of a midlife crisis. You and Jason built a life together and had a family together and he betrayed you and your children. I'm sorry that I broke up with you, but what happened between us wasn't in any way the same as what happened between you and Jason."

Camille drew a shaky breath. Max was probably right, but now wasn't the time to think about that. "As I said, I'm doing okay on my own," she replied before she got to her feet and walked away.

CHAPTER 12

*C*amille was just climbing into bed when the phone rang. It was after ten o'clock which was immediately worrying.

"Hello?"

"Hey, it's Jason. I just wanted to invite you and the kids to dinner tomorrow night," he said breezily.

"You're drunk."

"A little bit. I've been having fun with my old friend Max."

"Really? Before or after he got ice cream?"

"What?"

"Never mind. What time tomorrow?"

"Oh, I don't know. Six? How's that for you?"

"Where?"

"Come to the Riverside. They have a nice restaurant here."

"I'll bring the children, but I won't be staying."

"Oh, come on. Don't be like that. We have a lot to talk about. Brandon is going to be looking at colleges soon. We need to have a family discussion about the various possibilities."

Camille sighed. "Six o'clock at the Riverside. We'll be there." She put the phone down and slid under the covers. Part of her wanted to cry, but mostly she wanted to scream. Now that she knew for certain that she was over Jason, she really didn't want to see him or spend time with him. Her feelings for Max were considerably more confused.

Closing her eyes, she began to count sheep, determined not to stop until she fell asleep.

* * *

WHEN HER ALARM woke her at seven, she couldn't remember getting much past ten.

"I'm doing better," she told her reflection in the bathroom mirror. "I just need to stay away from Max." Her mirror image made a face at her. "And I need to stop talking to myself," she muttered as she got into the shower.

"We're having dinner with your father tonight," she told Molly over breakfast. "Tell your brother that when he gets up."

"What time and where?" Molly wanted to know.

"Six at the Riverside."

"He's not going to want to go."

"I don't want to go either, but we need to have a family discussion about colleges and Brandon's future."

"Does that mean that I don't have to go?"

"It's going to be a family discussion," Camille told her.

She grabbed her laptop and the paperwork from yesterday and headed into work. The kids could entertain themselves while she was out. She didn't expect Jason to get in touch, not when they had plans for later, but just in case, she'd given the kids strict orders to call her if they did hear from the man.

"I'm home and I'm late," she announced a few minutes after five as she burst through the house's front door.

"I don't want to go," Brandon said as a greeting.

"It's your future we're going to discuss," Camille replied. "You won't be happy if we make decisions without your input."

"I don't believe that Dad is actually going to be around in my future," Brandon countered.

"Let's see what he has to say over dinner," Camille suggested.

She ran up to her bedroom and changed into a summery dress and low heels. It only took her a few minutes to touch up her makeup. The restaurant at the Riverside was one of the fanciest places there was to eat in Ramsey and she'd never go there without putting some effort into her appearance, no matter who she was meeting.

Molly stuck her head around the door as Camille reached for her lipstick. "Do I look okay?" she asked her mother.

Camille smiled. "You look beautiful," she said.

Molly was wearing the only dress she owned. It was light grey on the top but it darkened gradually to black at the hem. Molly wore it for every special occasion.

"Brandon wants to wear jeans," Molly warned her before she disappeared.

Deciding it wasn't worth the fight, Camille didn't say a word about Brandon's appearance when she found him in the living room a short while later. "Ready to go?" she asked.

"Yes," he replied, getting to his feet.

At least he was wearing clean jeans and a polo shirt, Camille thought as they headed for the door.

The Riverside had valet parking, but Camille opted to park her car herself before they'd reached the valet stand. Then she led the children into the huge and lavishly decorated lobby.

"We're joining Jason Quinn for dinner," she told the host at the restaurant's entrance.

"Oh, yes, right this way," he replied.

Camille and the children followed him through the dining room to a separate room that Camille had never noticed before. The host held the door open for them to enter. Inside the small room, Max, Jason, and Seth were standing near a small bar.

"What an unexpected surprise," Camille said stiffly.

Jason turned around and smiled brightly at her. "You know I want to spend as much time with my buddy Max as I can," he said loudly. He carefully set his drink on the bar and then rushed over to them. He pulled Molly into a tight hug.

"Baby girl," he said. "It's so good to see you again. You look so grown up tonight."

"You just saw me yesterday," Molly replied as she stepped backward.

"Oh, yes, of course, but Brandon, look at you. You've grown up since the last time I saw you," Jason said, holding out a hand to shake hands with his son.

Brandon reached out and barely touched his father's hand. Jason raised an eyebrow and then turned to Camille.

"And my darling former wife. You look more beautiful than ever." He moved to embrace her, but she stepped sideways, heading for the bar.

"I didn't expect to see you two here," she said to Seth.

He shrugged. "Jason invited us."

"I thought it would be fun to have Max and Sam here," Jason yelled as he walked back to the bar.

"Seth," Max corrected him.

"What?" Jason asked.

"My assistant is called Seth, not Sam," Max said patiently.

Jason shrugged. "I didn't really want to invite him, but he seems to go everywhere with you."

Max laughed. "Seth works for me, but we're also friends."

"And Max is always working," Seth added.

"I thought you were retired," Jason said.

"I'm retired from the day to day running of the business, but I still own the business," Max countered.

Jason shrugged. "Have a drink," he told Camille.

"I'm driving," she replied.

"I can drive home," Brandon offered.

"There you are, have a drink," Jason said.

"Brandon only has a permit. If he drives, I have to supervise and that takes even more concentration than driving myself," Camille countered.

"As I understand it, you aren't very good at it," Jason laughed. "You let him hit Max, after all."

"It was my fault," Brandon said. "Mom told me to turn more tightly, but I didn't listen."

Jason shrugged and then downed what was left in his drink. "I need a drink, anyway."

"Let's order dinner," Max suggested. He handed Camille and the children menus and they quickly told the man behind the bar what they wanted. Max and Seth added their orders and, eventually, Jason chose something, seemingly at random.

"Let's sit down," Max said as the man typed their requests into the tablet behind the bar.

Camille crossed to the table and slid into a chair. "Molly, sit here," she said, waving to the chair on her right. Brandon dropped into the chair on her left.

Jason sat down next to Brandon with Max on his other side. Seth sat next to Max as Jason cleared his throat.

"Son, it's time for you to start thinking about your future," he said seriously.

"I have been thinking about my future. While I'd love to go to college in the city, it makes more sense for me to go to

Hailwood. Mom reckons she can put me through Hailwood without me having to take out any loans."

Jason shook his head. "You need to dream bigger. Your mother has never left Ramsey. She's missing out on an entire world of opportunities. I don't want her to ruin your life by keeping you here."

"I'm not making him stay forever," Camille interjected. "I just want him to get his degree before he leaves. It makes sound financial sense."

"I took out loans for my degree," Jason countered.

"And you were still paying them off when we got married," Camille reminded him.

He shook his head. "Whatever. I'm sure Brandon will be happier in the city with me."

"Are you suggesting that he should live with you?" Camille demanded.

"Oh, well, I mean, there isn't room in my apartment for anyone else, but I could help him find a place, for sure."

Camille sighed. Before she could speak again, a waiter arrived with their appetizers. No one spoke as they were served.

"Delicious," Seth said a moment later.

"I've never had a bad meal here," Camille told him.

"Eat here often, do you?" Jason asked. "I mean, you keep telling me that I should be sending you money, but if you can afford to eat here, you must be doing okay."

Camille just looked at him for a moment and then went back to eating.

"Or maybe you're here a lot because you're dating lots of different men," Jason said after a moment. "Is your mom dating anyone special?" he asked Molly.

Molly flushed. "Mom hasn't been out on a date since you left," she said flatly.

"There probably aren't too many single men in Ramsey,"

Jason said thoughtfully. "Maybe it's time you moved away," he suggested.

Camille counted to ten before she replied. "I'm quite happy here and quite happy on my own," she told him.

"Who does anyone root for in football?" Seth asked loudly.

"Camille always insisted on supporting the Dolphins," Jason replied. "I never understood it, but they were always her favorite team."

Camille blushed and looked down at the table. When she and Max had first started dating, they'd decided together that they'd support the Dolphins over any other team. It had been a joint act of rebellion against their friends and families, all of whom supported the Bills from nearby Buffalo.

"Max, too," Seth said. He looked at Camille and then shrugged. "What about baseball?" he asked.

"I don't follow baseball," Camille told him.

The food was delicious and Seth did his best to keep the conversation flowing, but the entire evening was difficult for Camille. Jason told them a few stories about his life in the city that only managed to make him seem even more selfish and shallow. By the time they'd eaten dessert, Camille was more than ready to leave.

"We haven't made any decisions about Brandon's future," Jason protested as she got up to go.

"It's far too soon to make any decisions," she replied. "It's something we're going to have to discuss many times over the next few years."

"I'm going back to the city tomorrow," Jason told her. "I'm starting a new job next week."

"You're leaving already?" Molly asked, tears springing into her eyes.

"I can't let my new employer down," Jason replied. "You

and Brandon should come and visit me in the city soon, though."

"Congratulations on the new job," Camille said.

"You'll let the children come for a visit, won't you?" Jason demanded.

"We'll have to see," she replied. "They have school and other commitments."

Jason waved a hand. "Spending time with their father is more important than school," he said.

Camille didn't bother to argue. Instead, she picked up her handbag and headed for the door. It was highly unlikely that Jason would ever follow through on the invitation, anyway.

Max followed her to the door. "Are you okay?" he asked.

She looked up at him and shrugged. "Again, I'm disappointed for the children."

"I want to…" Max began.

"You two seem awfully friendly," Jason called from his seat at the table. "I thought you told me once that you'd never forgive Max for what he did to you," he added with a malicious grin.

"Molly, Brandon, let's go," Camille snapped.

She didn't look back as she stormed out of the room, feeling angry at the world. The children were silent on the drive home.

"Are you okay?" she asked them as they walked into the house.

"I can't believe he's leaving already," Molly said with tears streaming down her face.

"He got a job. He needs to take it," Camille told her.

"He didn't even say goodbye properly," Molly complained.

"At least you got to have a fun afternoon at the zoo with him," Camille reminded her.

"Yeah, that's a lot more than I got," Brandon said sullenly.

Camille pulled him into a hug. "Your father has a lot of

things he needs to work through. His parents forced him to do certain things and now he's enjoying being able to make his own choices and do his own thing."

"He should have done his own thing before he had children," Molly said.

"Yes, well, that would have been better for everyone, really, but that isn't how things worked out," Camille replied.

She sent them upstairs to get ready for bed and then spent half an hour with each of them, talking about how they felt about everything that had happened. When she crawled into bed, she was reasonably certain that the children still felt loved and that they'd get over their father's latest bad behavior. As she reached for the light switch, the phone rang.

"I just wanted to say goodbye," Jason told her. "I truly am going to make more of an effort to be a part of the children's lives. This job is going to be a good thing for all of us."

"Great," Camille said, not believing a single word.

"You need to be careful of Max, though," Jason continued. "I saw how he was looking at you tonight. He wants you back, at least in the short term."

"I'm not interested."

"You say that now, but he's not going to give up easily. Max is used to getting what he wants. I wanted to ask you out in high school, but you were already Max's girl. We all knew better than to try to talk to you."

"Thanks for the warning, but it isn't necessary."

"He's only here because his mother is unwell," Jason continued. "She's having trouble with her memory and she needs full-time care. Maybe that's why Max is being so nice to you. Maybe he wants to marry you so that you can look after his mother."

Camille had to laugh. "Max has more than enough money to hire someone to look after his mother. I can't imagine him marrying anyone for any reason."

"I don't know. I think he sees you as a challenge. He's determined to get you back into his bed and I think he might be willing to marry you to accomplish that."

"I think you had too much to drink tonight."

"I did, but so did Max. He told me all about his mother and he let slip how he feels about you."

"Did he now?"

"He's upset that you're still angry with him and he's determined to seduce you before he goes back to the city. He'll dump you as soon as his mother is stable again, but he wants to have some fun before he goes."

"Thanks for the warning," she said again.

"You don't believe me."

"I don't care. I have no intention of getting involved with Max again."

"The thing is, this new job that I was offered? I'm going to be working for Max. He wants me out of Ramsey and away from you. He knows I still love you and that I want you back, so he offered me a job in the city to get me away from you."

"There's no way I would ever take you back."

"It would make the children happy."

She laughed. "And that's where I draw the line. I would do just about anything to make them happy, but taking you back, after everything you did to me, is a step too far."

"I never should have left."

"But now you're leaving again."

"Because of the job offer, not for any other reason. I was hoping to find a job in Ramsey. That's why I came back."

"I need to go. I wish you luck with your new job. I know the kids would like to hear from you more often."

"And you'd like more money," Jason chuckled. "I'll see what I can do."

She put the phone down and frowned at the receiver. At one time, she'd trusted Jason completely, never doubting anything he told her. That had changed once he'd started having affairs, but now she didn't know what to believe. Turning off the light, she pulled the covers over her head. It doesn't matter, she told herself. You just need to stay away from Max and everything will be fine.

* * *

JASON CALLED AGAIN the next morning and had a short conversation with each of the children in turn.

"He says he's going to call more often," Molly said when she was done speaking with him. "I hope he means it."

"I don't believe anything he told me," Brandon told Camille after his conversation with his father. "But at least he tried. It's more effort than he's made in the last five years, anyway."

"Take care of them for me," Jason said when Camille took the receiver. "I'm going to make more of an effort. I know I let you and the children down badly. I'll call you next week and let you know how the new job is going."

"That sounds good," Camille replied. She put the phone down and then sighed. She didn't believe anything he'd said, either, but she hoped to be proven wrong. Time would tell.

CHAPTER 13

*B*randon had to work at one, so she arranged to take her lunch hour so she could get him to work on time.

"This would be easier if I had my own car," he remarked as she drove.

"You don't have a license," she reminded him.

"I'm going to get it just as soon as I can."

"Let's take it one step at a time."

"Dave has his license and a car," Brandon told her. "He said when I saw him at Bessie's the other night that we should go out sometime."

"I'm not sure I'm ready for you to be going out with your friends doing the driving."

"Mom, I'm sixteen. You have to let me grow up sometime."

She'd pulled up at the Tae Kwon Do school while he'd been talking. He jumped out of the car and grabbed his bag before she could reply.

"I was hoping I had a few more years left before you grew up," she said softly to the empty seat.

When she got back to work, she rang Molly. "Is Mrs. Blake there?" she asked.

"Yes," Molly sighed. "Do you want to speak to her?"

"Not unless there's something I need to know."

"She's watching afternoon television, which is dire. I thought maybe I'd call Katie and see if she wants to come over."

"You can have one friend over, but only one."

"I know, I know."

When Camille got home from work not long after five, Katie was waiting at the door.

"My parents are going to be here any minute," she told Camille. "We're going out for dinner tonight to celebrate my dad's birthday."

"Have fun," Camille told her. The words were barely out of her mouth when Katie's mother's car pulled up on the driveway.

"Bye, Molly," Katie called over her shoulder as she ran out the door.

"Molly? Why aren't you down here saying goodbye to your guest?" Camille shouted up the stairs.

"Sorry," Molly said. "I dropped my phone behind my bed and I was trying to get it out. Katie didn't mind."

"It's still rude."

"Sorry."

"Brandon texted to say that Master Caldwell got pizza for all of the summer camp staff tonight. He's going to stay and eat and then take a class or maybe two. That means it's just us for dinner tonight," Camille told Molly.

"Let's go to the Diner," Molly suggested.

"What about the Ramsey Inn? We haven't been there for a while." She didn't really want to spend the money on eating out again, but she hadn't been grocery shopping in several days and she didn't have the energy to shop and cook after her long day at work.

"That's fine. I'll go and get ready."

After dinner, they picked up Brandon and went home.

"There are lights on in the Alexander mansion," Molly said as they drove down their street.

"At this hour?" Camille exclaimed. "Maybe I'll call Mrs. Blake and have her call Stanley."

"Or you could just call the police yourself," Brandon suggested.

Camille shrugged. "It doesn't feel like an emergency. There could be a perfectly logical explanation for it."

"I didn't think the house even had power," Molly said.

As they climbed out of the car, Camille looked over at the huge house next door. She couldn't see much of it, but she could see light coming from several of the windows. As she turned to go inside, someone called her name.

"Camille?"

She spun around and then let out a sigh of relief. "Seth? What brings you out here tonight?"

"I was just going around the Alexander mansion with Max's realtor. He saw your car drive by and suggested that I come over and let you know what was happening. He seemed to think that you might call the police if you noticed that there were lights on in the house."

"I did notice and I was going to call the police," she replied.

Seth nodded. "Well, there's no need. It's just me and the realtor and we're very nearly done, anyway."

"No Max?" Camille asked, trying to sound casual.

"Not yet, anyway. He may be here before we finish, but that seems unlikely at this point."

"What's it like inside?" she had to ask. "I've always wanted to see the inside of the place."

"Come and have a look," he suggested. "The realtor won't mind."

"Oh, I couldn't," she gasped.

"Oh, Mom, can we?" Molly asked.

Seth laughed. "You're all more than welcome. Come and have a look, but be very careful. It's in pretty bad condition."

Half an hour later, Camille and the children had toured the entire house.

"Thank you so much," she told Seth when they found him in what had once been the grand entryway to the mansion.

The sparkling chandelier was missing over half of its lights and crystals and only two of the remaining bulbs were lit. Wallpaper was peeling from every wall and the carpet was torn and stained. In spite of all of that, Camille could see how beautiful the house had once been.

"Is Max going to buy this house?" Molly asked.

Seth shrugged, glancing at the realtor who was clearly very interested in the answer. "I don't think he's decided yet," he told Molly.

"The smart thing to do would be to tear it down," the realtor told Seth. "It's a large lot. Mr. Steward could build his dream home in the same footprint for less than it would cost to bring this back to its former glory."

"Is that a possibility?" Camille asked, horrified by the idea.

"The house isn't on any historical registers," the realtor told her.

"Well, it should be," Camille replied.

He shrugged. "The current owners just want it sold. They don't care what happens to it."

"Do you mind if I take one more quick look around?" Camille asked.

"Go ahead," Seth told her. "We're still waiting for Max."

"We're going to go home," Molly said. "We want to watch something on the television."

"Something I'd approve of?" Camille asked.

Molly rolled her eyes as Seth laughed. She told her mother the name of the show before Camille agreed that they could go.

"Enjoy your tour," the realtor said as Camille headed for the stairs. "It might well be your last chance to see the house still standing."

She was looking out the huge picture window in the master bedroom, staring down at the town she loved, when Max found her. He joined her at the window.

"Ramsey looks beautiful from up here," he said softly.

"It really does."

"What do you think of the house?"

"It's everything I always imagined it would be, but it's been so neglected that it makes me sad. I don't know if it's worth saving."

"I don't either. I'm going to have an expert go through it and see what he thinks a total renovation would cost."

"The realtor suggested that you should tear it down and build your dream home."

Max nodded. "Or maybe I'll look elsewhere."

"Jason said you weren't going to be in Ramsey for long."

"Jason said? I'm not sure where he got that idea from."

"He told me that you only came back because your mother isn't well."

"There may be some truth in that," Max admitted with a sigh. He waved a hand at the town below them. "Ramsey is a wonderful little town, but I left because I felt trapped here. I've only been back a short while, but I'm starting to remember how that felt. Everyone knows everyone and sometimes I think the gossips know what I'm going to do next before I do."

Camille chuckled. "I didn't think you'd stick around," she said softly.

"I'm not planning on leaving any time soon," he replied quickly. "I truly do want to make Ramsey my home again. Once I've found a place to live, I might do some traveling, though. Visiting other places will remind me of why I love Ramsey so much."

Camille shrugged. "I suppose I should thank you for giving Jason a job," she said, deliberately changing the subject.

"He told me he's ready to rejoin the workforce and he had a very impressive resume from before his, um, break."

"And now he's gone back to the city," she sighed.

"You sound disappointed."

"The kids miss him a great deal and he barely had time to see them while he was here."

Max stared at her for a moment and then shook his head. "I'm sorry that he didn't stay longer," he said eventually.

The reply confused Camille. "He left because of his new job."

"Have dinner with me tomorrow night."

"What?"

"Have dinner with me tomorrow night," he repeated himself. "I want to get to know you again."

"We've had this conversation before. I'm not interested in getting to know you again, especially not now, when you've admitted you aren't planning on staying and you've driven Jason away."

"It was just meant to be dinner, not a lifetime commitment," Max snapped.

"Because you don't do lifetime commitments. Believe me, I know that."

"I wasn't ready for marriage thirty years ago."

"And it was your loss."

"Yes, it was," he agreed. "I've dated a lot of women in the years since I left Ramsey and I've never fallen in love again.

Maybe I'm still in love with you. Maybe we should find out."

He pulled her into his arms and stared into her eyes. "This feels so familiar," he whispered. "I don't want to do anything you don't want me to do."

"Then stop," she replied.

"Do you really want me to stop?" he asked, lowing his head until his lips were just a fraction of an inch above hers.

"One kiss," she murmured. "For old times' sake."

The room exploded with fireworks and shooting stars or maybe it just felt that way to Camille. Her knees went weak and she leaned into Max for support as the kiss continued. For what could have been five minutes or five hours, she got lost in the searing heat that excited and terrified her in equal measure.

When Max lifted his head, he raised an eyebrow. "Pleasant enough for you?" he asked.

"It was overwhelming," she admitted. "But I still won't have dinner with you tomorrow."

"What about the next day?"

She laughed and then took a small step backward, out of his embrace. It felt cold and lonely there and for a moment she was tempted to return to his arms. "I'm too old to play games," she said firmly.

"I'm not playing games."

"I've been hurt too badly in the past to believe that," she told him. "I don't trust anyone anymore."

"And you won't give me a chance to prove to you that I've changed?"

"Did you ever think about me over the last thirty years?"

"I thought about you a lot. I thought about coming back for you, too, but then you married Jason and ended that dream."

"You had ten years after you left to come back for me

before I married Jason. You can't seriously be suggesting that you thought I'd wait for you forever?"

He shook his head. "Those ten years went by so fast," he sighed. "Actually, the last thirty years have gone past far too quickly. When I left, I thought I'd visit, but my father preferred to visit me in the city. He'd always wanted to live there, you know. Mom was the one who insisted on living in Ramsey."

"I didn't know that."

"They used to visit me three or four times a year, as often as my father could convince my mother to come, really. I didn't have any reason to come back to Ramsey."

"Ouch."

He chuckled. "I didn't mean that the way it sounded. I missed you and I never stopped caring about you, but I convinced myself that there were plenty of other women out there. Besides, I knew if we got back together that you'd want to stay in Ramsey forever and that wasn't in my plans. I saw how unhappy my father was, living here to make my mother happy. I didn't want that for myself."

Camille nodded. "I'm glad you found what you wanted in the city."

"I love living in New York. It's vibrant and alive in a way that only one of the biggest cities in the world can be. I worked hard and made some money and then I got really lucky and turned some money into a lot of money. No amount of money can make my mother well again, though."

"I'm sorry."

"She's having problems with her memory and she's finding it very upsetting. I have nurses living with her twenty-four, seven, but she doesn't want them there. She'd rather be on her own, but when she is, she leaves pots boiling on the stove or takes a walk and forgets how to get home again."

"I'm very, very sorry," Camille said, putting a hand on his arm.

"I'm fortunate that I can afford to hire people to help, but she really wants me with her all the time. She remembers me, at least for now, but she doesn't always remember that I'm an adult. She nags me to do my homework and sends me to bed at nine o'clock."

"Do you think she would remember me?"

"I don't know. I've been trying to keep her at home, away from everyone, because it's all so difficult, but maybe she'd do better if she were allowed to do more, as long as she had close supervision. Maybe a visitor would be good for her."

"I'm working all week, but I could visit on Saturday," Camille offered.

"Let me think about it," Max said. "A lot will depend on how she's doing, really. She has good days and bad days."

"Let me know. I always liked your mother, but I haven't really seen her since you left Ramsey."

"She always liked you, too. She told me when I left that I was a fool for not waiting for you to graduate and then taking you with me."

Camille shrugged. "She said the same to me," she said softly. Max's mother had also insisted that Max would come to his senses one day and come back for her, too, a hope she'd clung to for nearly a decade.

"Maybe we could talk more about her and Saturday over dinner tomorrow," Max suggested.

"Seriously? You're still trying?"

"I am, and I'm going to keep trying until you say yes."

"I'm not going to say yes."

"One dinner and then, if you tell me you don't want to see me again, I'll stop asking," he promised.

"I'm not interested in getting back together."

"That's fine. I really just want to talk. I want to hear all about your life over the past thirty years."

"We could do that over a quick drink. I've not done anything interesting."

"I don't believe that. You had two amazing children, at the very least. You can tell me every funny story you have about them."

She shook her head. "I'd rather hear about your life. You've been all over the world and you've met famous people. I want to hear about that."

"So you'll have dinner with me?"

"I, that is, oh, why not," she sighed. "I feel as if you tricked me into that somehow."

He shrugged. "I'd rather believe that I charmed you into it."

"Whatever, just remember that it's only dinner and only this one time. The whole town will be talking about us, regardless."

"I don't care what they say."

"I have to care, though. What they say might just upset Molly and Brandon."

"We'll take our own cars to the restaurant and make sure that we leave separately so that no one thinks we're sleeping together," he suggested.

She shrugged. "That may help, anyway."

"Where do you want to go?"

"I don't care."

"The Riverside it is," he replied. "They have the best food in the area."

"I'm sure you've had much better."

"But not in such wonderful company."

She rolled her eyes. "Please, save those sort of lines for women who will believe them."

"I did miss you," he said. He closed the small gap between

them and cupped her chin in his hand, tipping her head up. "One more kiss before we go," he whispered.

"Max?" Seth's shout interrupted them only a moment later.

"I'll be there in a minute," Max called back. "I may have to fire him," he said to Camille.

She laughed. "I need to get home anyway. The children will be destroying the house."

"I'll see you at the Riverside at six," he reminded her as they walked down the stairs together. She walked slowly, trying to memorize every detail of the old home as they went.

"See you at six," she agreed at the front door.

While he offered her a ride home, she was more than happy to walk. The kids were still watching television when she got back. Neither of them had to be up the next morning, so she left them to their program and headed to bed. She had to work in the morning, after all.

She was sorting the day's mail, trying to decide what to wear for her night out with Max when her cell phone rang. Frowning, she pulled it out of her pocket. Only a very select few people had the number and they all knew to only use it in emergencies. She didn't recognize the caller's number.

"Hello?"

"Camille, it's Max. I got Molly to give me your number. I'm really sorry, but something has come up at my office in New York. I'm leaving now to deal with it. Can we reschedule our dinner for another day, please?"

She took a deep breath before she replied. "Sure, no problem. Call me when you get back," she said, ending the call before he could reply.

Why had she ever believed that he had changed? He didn't want to be in Ramsey and he clearly wasn't retired, either, no matter what he'd said. She wasn't sure if she wanted to cry or scream or both. At least you found out the truth before you fell in love again, a little voice in her head said. Except she knew better. She'd never stopped loving Max and after last night she felt as head over heels about him as she had after their very first kiss when she'd been fourteen.

CHAPTER 14

"*Y*ou're better company, anyway," she told Terri over burgers at the Diner that evening.

Terri laughed. "I know you don't mean it, but thanks anyway."

"I do mean it. You're my friend and I know I can trust you, unlike some people."

Terri nodded and then frowned. "Have you ever had a female friend let you down?" she asked.

"What do you mean?"

"I mean, women can sometimes be just as unreliable as men."

"There's a difference between a girlfriend cancelling plans at the last minute and a man leaving you after six years together."

"Yes, but maybe it's just possible that you're being a bit hard on Max."

"He's only here because of his mother. He offered Jason a job in New York that made him go away again. He's supposed to be retired, but he rushed away for work. He broke my heart thirty years ago."

"And that last one is the biggest problem," Terri suggested.

"I'm over it."

"Why does it matter if he only came back because of his mother?"

Camille sighed. "I just wish he'd come back because he missed Ramsey, because he wants to be here, not because he feels he has to be here."

"He's here. Surely that's what matters."

"He isn't here, though. He's back in New York City, running his multi-billion dollar business."

"You should be happy he has a job," Terri suggested.

Camille made a face. "Stop being sensible and logical. I'm mad at him and I don't want you to take his side."

"I'm not taking his side. I'm simply trying to help you see things from a different perspective."

"It doesn't matter. I've decided that, when he comes back, if he comes back, that I don't want to see him. My life is complicated enough without him in it. We were only ever going to be friends, anyway."

"And you have more than enough friends," Terri said.

Camille frowned. "Why are you arguing with me tonight?"

"I thought I was agreeing with you."

"And I'm being unreasonable and difficult. Why do you put up with me?"

"Because I don't have enough friends," Terri laughed. "I have a very dull life and your adventures with Max let me live vicariously. Do you know how long it's been since I've been kissed, truly properly kissed?"

"You've been divorced for three years. Maybe it's time for you to start dating again."

"I don't know. I'm not sure I'm ready to go back out there and deal with men and their egos and their issues."

Camille laughed. "It's hard to imagine how our species has survived this long, really. Men and women do seem to have come from different planets."

"But we're talking about your problems, not mine," Terri said. "If Max buys the Alexander mansion, you'll be neighbors."

"He isn't going to buy the Alexander mansion. He's probably not going to stay in the area. Let's talk about work."

"That's a bit extreme. I'm sure we can find things to talk about besides Max and work."

"The weather has been good lately," Camille offered.

"I'm looking forward to the new school year. I always start out incredibly optimistic about how the year is going to go. This year the kids will be interested and engaged. The administration will truly listen to teacher input and will actively support us. The parents will take an active role in their children's educations and be helpful without smothering said children."

"You forget 'and the support staff will continue to do their amazing and awe-inspiring job every single day, especially Camille in the main office,'" Camille reminded her.

Terri laughed. "That, too."

"But now we're talking about work."

"Have you met the new math teacher yet?" Terri asked.

"I have. He seems really nice, but I'm not sure how he ended up in Ramsey."

The pair chatted about various work colleagues over dinner and dessert.

"That was delicious," Camille said as she pushed her empty chocolate cake plate away from her.

"I shouldn't have had dessert," Terri sighed. "In spite of what I said earlier, I am thinking about dating again. I need to lose twenty pounds first, though."

"No you don't. You need to embrace your beautiful body and get out there. If a man only cares about you when you weigh a certain amount, he isn't worth having."

"I know you're right, but I'll feel more confident if I lose a few pounds."

"Lose them for you, then, but don't use that as an excuse to hide away."

"We'll see."

"Are you going to try online dating?"

"I don't know what to try. There don't seem to be any single men around my age in Ramsey."

"There's Seth," Camille suggested.

"He's too young and he's too busy. I don't want a man who works all the time."

"I think Douglas Holloway is single, but you'll probably say the same about him."

"Oh, definitely. Lucas Hogan works the poor man to death. I don't know why he puts up with it, really."

"I believe Mr. Hogan pays him well."

"No doubt, but I'd rather find a man who has some balance between his life and his work. I love my job, but I also love leaving the school and not thinking about it in evenings."

"Except you're the advisor for four different afterschool clubs," Camille pointed out.

"After school and after the clubs, then."

"What about homework? You always seem to be marking homework when we talk during the week."

Terri laughed. "Maybe I need to work on my work/life balance, too."

They walked out to their cars together.

"Thanks for joining me at the last minute," Camille said when they reached her car. "I didn't want to sit home alone tonight and the kids both had plans with their friends."

"I wasn't doing anything. Thomas is staying at his father's house until school starts. I would have made myself a can of soup and watched reruns of some eighties television show if I'd stayed home."

"I'm glad I called, then. Those shows weren't good in the eighties."

"There were some excellent programs made in the eighties," Terri argued. "I should know. I watch them all when Thomas is with his father."

"And I never get to watch anything I want to watch in my house. The kids always have control of the television when they're there. To be honest, I never think to put it on when they're out."

"You could go home and watch something now," Terri suggested.

"Maybe," Camille replied with a sigh. She climbed into her car and drove home slowly. Maybe she should watch something on TV, she thought as she parked. Or maybe she should read one of the books in the pile that she kept accumulating but never seemed to get around to reading.

She was halfway through a murder mystery when Molly got home.

"Did you have fun at Jen's?" Camille asked.

"I suppose so," Molly sighed.

"What happened?"

"She said something about you and Max, that's all."

"What about me and Max?"

"That you were spending a lot of time together and how did I feel about moving to New York City, because that was where we'd have to go if you and Max got married."

Camille sighed. "First of all, Max and I aren't getting married. We're barely even friends, really. We haven't been spending a lot of time together, either."

"You were going to have dinner together tonight."

"One dinner, for old times' sake, nothing more. We aren't getting married. At the moment, we aren't even speaking to one another."

"If you did get married, would we have to move to New York?"

"No, absolutely not. I have no intention of leaving Ramsey, not for Max or for anyone else."

"You wouldn't go with Dad when he wanted to go."

Camille was shocked. "You father didn't ask me to go with him," she said sharply.

"That isn't what he told me," Molly replied.

"What did he tell you?"

"It doesn't matter."

"It really does matter," Camille countered. "I won't let him fill your head with half-truths."

"He just said that when he first started talking about moving to the city you told him that he'd have to go on his own if he really wanted to go. He made it sound as if he really wanted all of us to move with him, but you refused."

"When he first mentioned going, he was planning to take someone else with him," Camille told her.

"Who?"

Camille sighed. "It might be easier if we skip over that part."

"I'm home," Brandon shouted as he walked into the house. He looked surprised when he saw Molly and Camille in the living room.

"We noticed," Molly said dryly.

"How was the movie?" Camille asked.

He shrugged. "It was okay, but we want to see *Zombie Frogs from the Ninth Dimension* on Saturday, if we can."

Camille made a face. "Where is it showing?"

"In Saunders," Brandon replied, naming the slightly larger, neighboring town. "Dave can drive."

"We'll see," Camille told him, knowing that she'd say yes eventually. She knew Dave's family well enough to know that he'd be a careful driver.

"But we were talking about Dad," Molly said.

Camille had been hoping she'd forgotten about that. "Let's just say that he may not have told you the entire story," she replied.

"What did he tell you?" Brandon asked.

"He said that Mom refused to move to New York City with him when he wanted to move there. He said she was the one who split up the family," Molly replied.

Camille took a deep breath, reminding herself that whatever she thought of Jason, he was still Molly and Brandon's father. "That isn't quite right," she said after a moment.

"Did you refuse to move with him?" Molly asked.

"As I said earlier, he had other plans," Camille said.

"He was going to move with his girlfriend," Brandon told Molly.

"Dad had a girlfriend?" Molly looked shocked.

"Yeah, her name was Darlene and she was like twenty-five and dumb as a stump," Brandon replied.

Camille couldn't help but laugh. "Without going into too many details, Brandon is correct. Your father's initial plan was to move to New York with a woman named Darlene."

"Why didn't I know that, but Brandon did?"

"He brought Darlene with him when he picked me up from school one day," Brandon told her. "He swore me to secrecy though. He said Mom wasn't to know about her."

"But you did know, didn't you?" Molly asked Camille.

"Ramsey is a small town, so, yes, I did know. I knew before Brandon told me, and then he told me all about her once he got home that day, as well."

"Good for you," Molly told her brother.

"I didn't want to have secrets from Mom. It didn't feel

right," Brandon said with a shrug. "Anyway, they were talking about moving away. Darlene said she hated Ramsey and couldn't wait to go and Dad was all excited about starting over in a big city where he could reinvent himself any way he wanted."

"What happened to Darlene?" Molly wanted to know.

Camille sighed. Maybe it was time to stop trying to shield the children from all of the things that had gone wrong with her marriage, especially considering Jason was telling Molly things that weren't true.

"Your father started seeing Darlene about a year before he moved to New York," she told Molly.

"But you and Dad were still married then," Molly protested.

"And eventually, Darlene got tired of your father saying he was going to leave me and move to the city, so she ended things. At least, that's the story that I heard through the grapevine," Camille said.

Brandon sat down on the couch next to her. "Are you okay to talk about this?" he asked.

"I've never really talked about what happened with you guys. It was between your father and me and it's important to me that you have a good relationship with him, regardless of our issues," she replied.

"Except Dad was happy to tell me that everything was your fault," Molly protested. "We should know the truth."

"I can't tell you the truth," Camille protested. "I can only tell you my side of the story."

"I think that's more likely to be closer to the truth than anything Dad says," Brandon remarked.

Camille shrugged. "Your father had a difficult childhood. His parents put a lot of pressure on him to do certain things and he never rebelled against that. When they passed away, he seemed to feel as if he was suddenly free to do all of the things he'd always wanted to do."

"Including sleeping with much younger women," Brandon said sharply.

"So what happened next?" Molly asked. "Darlene broke up with him and then what happened?"

"There were other women. I didn't bother to keep track of them. Your father moved into the spare room and we started talking about separating. My father got sick and a lot of my time and attention went to him and to my mother. I did my best to keep you guys from realizing how bad things were, but I'm sure your father felt a bit abandoned."

"Except he was already cheating," Molly said.

"Whatever he was doing before, when my father passed away, your father seemed to suddenly realize that life was short. He had a long list of things he'd always wanted to do and he'd inherited some money when his parents died. We were going to put a new roof on the house and put some money away for you guys for college, but your father decided that he wanted to use the money for other things."

"Things for himself," Brandon muttered.

"He wanted to do all of the things that he used to dream of doing back when his parents were alive and he was doing everything he could to please them," Camille told him.

"Why are you making excuses for him? He cheated on you and then he decided to leave you and me and Molly," Brandon said angrily. "He left and he used our college money to pay for trips and fun and he never gave us a single thought."

"He said he thinks about us all the time," Molly protested.

"He never sends any money to help Mom, though," Brandon snapped.

"He said he does, though," Molly said. "He said he's been sending money for Mom to put away for college."

"Is he?" Brandon demanded.

Camille sighed. "He sent a hundred dollars a month for the first three months after he left. I haven't had a penny from him since," she said quietly.

Brandon cursed loudly. "I hate him," he shouted.

"You have every right to be angry with him," Camille said. "And you have every right to not be angry, too," she told Molly. "You're both old enough to understand that there are two sides to every story. You should hear your father's side before you decide what to believe."

"I heard his side," Molly told her. "He told me that he decided that he needed a change and that he wanted to move away and you refused to go. He never mentioned any other women."

"For what it's worth, if he had asked me to move to New York City with him, I would have refused," Camille replied. "I wouldn't have wanted to move you and Brandon away from the schools here. Living in a big city would have been a big adjustment for both of you and for me. I didn't want to make that adjustment."

"He never asked, though, did he?" Molly asked.

Camille shrugged. "Not that I recall. I think I would remember, but I have blocked out a lot of our arguments. It was a very difficult time and we used to have screaming fights in whispers in the kitchen while you two and my parents were all asleep."

"If you didn't want to go, he should have stayed here," Brandon said. "Regardless, he's the one who hasn't been back to visit in five years. He's the one who never calls and never sends any money. Whatever he tells Molly, his actions speak louder than words."

"I don't want to see him again," Molly said as tears rolled down her cheeks.

"I doubt that will be a problem." Brandon said darkly.

"He told me he's ready to make changes in his life," Camille told them. "He's got a job now, anyway."

"When he starts sending money, let me know," Brandon said. "I'm going to go to bed."

Molly buried her head in a pillow, sobbing quietly as Brandon left the room. Camille sat with her daughter, talking quietly, until Molly was calm again. Then she went up and had a long talk with Brandon, reminding him that she loved him more than anything. When she crawled into bed, she shed a few tears of her own before she fell into a restless sleep.

* * *

THE NEXT DAY seemed to drag past, with Camille looking forward to the long weekend that would mark the end of summer. On Saturday morning she made pancakes for breakfast.

"You should do this every Saturday," Brandon suggested as he shoveled pancakes dripping in syrup into his mouth.

"I won't promise, but I'll try," she said. "We'll make it a new tradition."

"I love this new tradition," Molly laughed.

Half an hour later, Dave came to pick up Brandon for the movies.

"We'll be back around two," Brandon told her. "We're going to get lunch on the way back."

Camille nodded. "Have fun."

She and Molly spent the morning organizing Molly's closet, a job that Molly was supposed to have done over the summer. They still had work to do when they stopped for lunch. Camille was putting sandwiches on the table when someone knocked on the door.

"Mrs. Blake? I didn't call…" she began when she saw the

woman on her doorstep. She trailed off as her eyes shifted to the man standing behind Mrs. Blake. "Stanley? Oh, no. Brandon?"

CHAPTER 15

*M*rs. Blake pulled Camille into a hug as Stanley spoke. Most of the words didn't sink in, but certain words and phrases jumped out at her.

"ran a red light"

"other driver didn't stop"

"both boys are at Ramsey General"

"badly shaken up but expected to make full recoveries"

"They're going to be okay?" Camille demanded when Stanley was done.

"The doctors are confident that they'll both be absolutely fine," Stanley assured her.

"Come on, then," Mrs. Blake said. "I came along so that I could drive you to the hospital. You don't want to drive and Stanley has to go and find that other driver. He or she should go to jail for a very long time, but we all know that won't happen."

Camille nodded. "I need my handbag," she said uncertainly.

"Here," Molly said, handing her mother the bag. "I put the sandwiches in the refrigerator and locked the back door."

"Thank you," Camille said, giving her daughter a hug.

"Let's go," Molly said. Camille could see Molly blinking back tears as they locked up the house and rushed to Mrs. Blake's car.

"He's going to be okay," she told Molly as they climbed into the backseat.

"He better be," she choked out.

Camille took a slow breath and told herself not to cry. She needed to be strong for Molly and for Brandon. Mrs. Blake pulled her car right up to the hospital entrance.

"No one will ticket me," she laughed as she slid into the no parking zone. "Stanley wouldn't have it. I'll go and park somewhere and you can find me in the lobby when you need a ride home."

Camille and Molly were out of the car as soon as it stopped. Karen Henderson-Archer was sitting behind the information desk wearing a volunteer nametag. "He's on two, in the pediatric unit," she called to Camille as she and Molly walked through the door. "And Camille? He's going to be fine."

Waving her thanks, Camille headed for the bank of elevators. When a car didn't appear immediately, she pushed open the door to the stairs and ran up them with Molly at her heels. The nurse on duty, Sharon McCall, was another former schoolmate.

"He's fine," Sharon said as a greeting. "He's in 212," she added. "And he's already been complaining about being in pediatrics. Apparently, he doesn't care for the décor."

Camille stopped in the doorway to the room and then laughed. Brandon was lying back on the bed, frowning at the cartoon animals that covered the walls.

"It wasn't Dave's fault," was the first thing he said to his mother.

"I know," she replied, letting a few tears slide down her cheeks as she crossed to the bed.

Molly pulled her brother into a fierce hug, tears flowing freely.

"Ouch, hey, be careful," he exclaimed.

"Sorry, not sorry," Molly said. "Stanley you could have been killed."

"But I wasn't. I'm fine, aside from maybe a concussion and a few internal injuries," he replied.

"Concussion? Internal injuries?" Camille repeated. "I don't like the sound of any of that."

"Camille?" Donald Archer said from the doorway. "Let's talk."

"Is he going to be okay?" she demanded as the doctor led her into a small conference room near the elevators.

"He should be absolutely fine, but we're going to keep him for twenty-four hours for observation. He was wearing his seatbelt and the airbag went off but he managed to hit his head on the door and his seatbelt left some pretty impressive marks across his chest and hips. He was in a lot of pain when he arrived and he's been given some meds to counter that. If he still needs that level of pain control tomorrow, we'll be keeping him another day," he told her.

She nodded. "How's Dave?" she asked.

He hesitated. "I'm sure everyone in Ramsey knows as much about his condition as I do," he said dryly after a moment. "The car that ran the red light hit the driver's side of the car. Luckily for Dave, he had side airbags as well as front ones. He's pretty banged up and he may have a broken arm from hitting the steering wheel, but all things considered, he came through it fairly well. I've seen pictures of the car and I can't believe that both boys walked away from the crash."

Camille let out a breath she hadn't realized she'd been holding. "Thank you," she said.

"He'll be in excellent hands here, but if you have any concerns, please don't hesitate to call me directly. We're all struggling through our kids' teen years together, after all."

She nodded. Whatever she thought of the man personally, she knew he was a good doctor and tonight he even seemed like a good person. When she got back to Brandon's room, he and Molly were snuggled on the bed together, watching television.

"You can't stay here," she told Molly.

"I don't want to stay here," Molly countered. "This bed is hard as a rock."

"So get out of it," Brandon suggested.

Molly climbed out carefully. "I just wanted you to feel loved," she told him.

"Thanks?" he said, making the word a question in a way that made both Molly and Camille laugh.

"Can I go home, too?" Brandon asked.

"They want to keep you overnight," she told him. "You got pretty banged up and you've also been given some strong pain medication."

He nodded. "I feel really, really, really happy," he said. "Nothing hurts, either."

"I think they need to dial back the meds," Camille muttered.

"Can you get me some pajamas?" he asked. "Even full of pain meds, this hospital gown is embarrassing."

Molly laughed. "I wasn't going to mention it, but it's awful."

"If you'll be okay on your own for a few minutes, I'll go home and pack you a suitcase," Camille told him. "I'd better call your father, too."

"Must you?" Brandon asked. "He isn't going to care."

"He still needs to know," Camille told him. "I'll be back soon."

"I told you he was fine," Mrs. Blake said from the doorway. "You take my car and get home and pack bags for yourself and Brandon. I assume you'll want to stay here tonight."

Camille nodded. "I do, but…" she trailed off as she looked at Molly.

"I'll stay with Molly," Mrs. Blake said. "While you've been visiting, I went home and packed my bags for a sleepover. I packed all my favorite lotions and potions for Molly to try. We'll get rid of the wrinkles she doesn't have and then we'll bake my favorite chocolate chip bar cookies and eat the entire pan of them ourselves."

Brandon made a noise that made both Molly and Mrs. Blake laugh.

"And then we'll make another pan of them so that Brandon can have some," Mrs. Blake added quickly. "I'll let her stay up far too late and tell her everything I can remember about what you were like as a child," she told Camille.

"I'm not sure I like that idea," Camille protested.

Molly grinned. "I do," she said quickly.

"I'll have Stanley follow you home. He can bring my car back here so I can take Molly back to your house. That way you can drive back with your car."

Nodding, Camille headed out with Mrs. Blake's keys. She drove home with Stanley right behind her. He took his mother's keys from her as soon as she'd parked the car.

"I'm going to leave the police car here for now," he told her, nodding to where he'd left it parked at the curb. "One of the other guys will drop me back off to get it later."

Inside, Camille packed a bag for herself and one for Brandon. She was on her way back to the hospital more quickly than she'd imagined possible. Back in pediatrics, she stopped to visit Dave who was sleeping under his mother's watchful eye. The two women both blinked away tears as they hugged before Camille made her way back to Brandon's room.

Brandon was fast asleep in spite of the volume on the television. Molly and Mrs. Blake left quietly when Camille entered. The first thing she did was turn off the television. Then she pulled out her cell phone. She found Jason's contact information and pressed the call button. It rang a dozen times before she gave up and disconnected.

Sighing, she stood up and paced back and forth, trying to decide what to do next. She didn't have any other phone numbers for the man, but maybe Max did. The problem was, she really didn't want to call Max. Over the next hour, she tried Jason's number a dozen times. Her stomach was growling and her head was starting to ache when she finally put her phone away and sat back down in the chair in the corner of the room.

"Mom?" Brandon said a few minutes later. "My head hurts." The words were barely out of his mouth when he started gagging.

Camille grabbed the plastic tub that was next to the bed and held it in front of him as he lost the contents of his stomach. When he paused for a moment, she pressed the bell to ring for help.

"Typical with head injuries," the nurse said. "We'll need to wake him every hour or so to assess him," she added. "It's going to be a long night."

She went and got another tub before taking away the one that Camille had used. "I'll check back in a little while," she told them. "I'll also check with the doctor to see if he's allowed anything else for pain."

With her own head pounding, Camille nodded and then found her handbag. Trying to hide what she was doing from her son, she dug out painkillers and swallowed two dry.

When she turned around, Brandon was lying back on the bed staring at her.

"Are you okay?" she asked.

"My head hurts," he replied. "And my stomach hurts and, well, just about everything hurts."

"Try to rest, at least for a little while."

"The nurse said you had to wake me every hour," he said tiredly.

"So sleep for fifty-nine minutes," she suggested.

"Did you talk to Dad?"

"He isn't answering his phone right now. He may be working."

"Or he may be off having fun and not giving a damn."

"Let's not have that conversation right now," she suggested. "Rest."

He sighed and then slowly shut his eyes. As his breathing slowed, Camille pulled out her phone again.

"Answer," she muttered as she listened to the phone ringing.

Sighing, she tapped over to her list of incoming calls. Max's number was at the top of the list. A quick look at Brandon had her pressing his number. She'd do anything for her kids, even call Max.

"Hello?"

"Max, it's Camille. I'm trying to reach Jason but he isn't answering the number I have for him. I was hoping you might have another number for him."

"What's wrong?" he asked, sounding concerned.

"Brandon was in a car accident. He's going to be fine, but he has a concussion and he's going to be in the hospital overnight."

"Are you staying with him?"

"Yes."

"What about Molly?"

"She's at home with Mrs. Blake."

Max chuckled. "And Mrs. Blake can deal with anything life throws at her, assuming she's still as formidable as she was when we were younger."

"She's a bit older, but otherwise exactly the same."

"I'm going to have to visit her when I get back. She used to babysit me when I was a child and I always did my best to make her life difficult. She'd already raised four boys, though. Nothing I did ever surprised her."

"Do you have a number for Jason?" Camille asked, not feeling like strolling down memory lane at the moment.

Max gave her a number that she didn't have.

"Thank you," she said.

"I'll call you when I get back to Ramsey," he told her.

"Don't bother," she replied. "I think I'm better off on my own." The words sounded harsh when they came out, but with her head still throbbing, she wasn't capable of being polite.

"Take care of yourself," Max said in a low voice before he hung up.

"Myself and everyone else," Camille muttered. She took several deep breaths before she dialed the number Max had given her.

"Hello?"

"Jason? It's Camille."

"This isn't the best time," he began.

"Brandon was in a car accident," she interrupted.

"Brandon? Was he driving? Is he okay?"

"He wasn't driving. His friend, Dave, was driving. They're both expected to recover, although Brandon will be in hospital overnight. He has a concussion."

"So he'll be fine?"

"Eventually."

"Well, that's good news."

"Jason?" Camille heard a female voice say. "The bed is lonely without you."

"I have to go," Jason said. "Tell Brandon that I'm happy he's going to be okay."

He ended the call before Camille could reply. She felt tears streaming down her cheeks as she put her phone into her pocket. Why had she ever married that man? A glance at Brandon reminded her that she had two very good reasons to be grateful to Jason. That didn't stop her heart from aching for the sake of her children, who were going to grow up without their father in their lives. She didn't get a chance to dwell on the thought, though, as Brandon woke up sick again.

The next several hours were a blur as Brandon continued to retch and gag long after his stomach had been emptied. Between bouts of nausea, he complained about pain, sleeping only fitfully. Around six, they brought him a light meal that he didn't want to eat. She found herself coaxing him to have a few bites of gelatin as if he were a small child again. He managed to eat enough to satisfy Camille. Now she just had to hope that it would stay down.

"Did you have any dinner?" one of the nurses asked Camille as they collected Brandon's tray.

"Not yet. I'll get something later," she replied vaguely, aware that she'd skipped lunch and that her headache was in danger of becoming a migraine if she didn't eat something soon.

"Do you have a friend you could call? Someone who could come and sit with Brandon for a few minutes while you eat?"

Camille shrugged. With Thomas at his father's, Terri had gone to visit an old friend for a few days. She'd be back just before school started. There wasn't anyone else she'd leave Brandon with, not when he was so miserable.

"We aren't allowed to go and get food for you, but you can order pizza and have it delivered to the lobby," the nurse suggested.

"I'll do that in a little while," Camille said. "Thank you."

Brandon dozed off as Camille paced back and forth. The thought of food made her feel queasy, but she knew she needed to eat. She really didn't want to leave her son, though.

Movement in the doorway made her quickly brush away a stray tear. She forced a smile onto her face as she waited for yet another nurse or aide to stick a head into the room.

"Max? What are you doing here?" she demanded as the last person she'd been expecting walked into the room.

He looked at her for a moment and then shrugged. "I'm not entirely sure," he said. "After we talked, I couldn't stop thinking about Brandon and about you. I was worried that you were here on your own, and I thought maybe I could help."

"I'm fine," she told him before she surprised them both by bursting into tears.

Max pulled her into his arms and held her close as she let out some of the shock and upset that she'd been trying to keep locked away. For a few minutes, she simply sobbed, but gradually she became aware of Max's arms around her and his hand, gently stroking the back of her head. When she realized that it was getting incredibly warm in the small room, she took a deep breath and then straightened and pulled away.

"I'm sorry," she said, blushing.

"You've nothing to be sorry about," he countered. "It's been a long and scary day."

She nodded. "But Brandon is going to be fine."

He took her chin in his hand and stared into her eyes. "You have a migraine, don't you?"

"How did you, I mean, yes, but I'm fine," she stammered.

"Did you take anything for it?"

"I'm fine."

He frowned at her. "I remember your migraines. When did you last eat something?"

She shrugged. "I missed lunch," she admitted.

"It's seven o'clock. You haven't eaten since breakfast?"

The concern on his face nearly took her breath away. "I was going to get something soon," she said, looking away.

"But you didn't want to leave Brandon on his own," he suggested.

"He needs someone with him, although I'm sure he'd deny that if he was awake."

"I'll stay with him. Go downstairs to the café and get something to eat."

She wanted to argue, but Max was right. If she didn't eat, she wasn't going to be able to look after Brandon properly.

"I'll be as quick as I can," she said as she grabbed her handbag.

"No rush. I can't see him being any trouble," Max replied.

"Famous last words," Camille muttered as she headed for the elevators.

* * *

When she returned to the floor twenty minutes later, having had a sandwich and a cold drink, she was feeling quite a bit better. The second dose of painkillers were starting to have an effect and she was no longer hungry. The sound of retching as she reached Brandon's room made her increase her pace.

Max was standing next to the bed, holding the plastic tub while Brandon moaned. From what Camille could see, he'd managed to throw up all over the bed, the floor, and Max.

Not sure if she should laugh or cry, she took a step toward the bed and then stopped.

"Have you rung for the nurse?" she asked.

Max looked at her and then shook his head. "I'm not sure where the call button went. Things got a little crazy for a minute."

Brandon looked over at his mother. "I woke up feeling really sick. I'm sorry about the mess."

"It isn't your fault," Max interjected. "I should have been quicker with the bucket."

Camille went back outside and found one of the aides. Within minutes, a pair of them had the room, the bed, and Brandon cleaned up. That just left Max looking a mess.

"I'm going to go home and take a shower and change," he told Camille. "I'll be back soon."

She opened her mouth to reply, but he'd already left the room.

"Why is he coming back?" Brandon asked.

"I have no idea," Camille replied.

amille and Brandon were watching television together when Max returned about thirty minutes later. He was carrying a small suitcase and a medium-sized box. After putting the suitcase down in a corner, he handed the box to Camille.

"Snacks," he said. "And some things to keep us busy."

Camille lifted the lid and discovered boxes of crackers and cookies, bars of chocolate, a loaf of bread and jars of peanut butter and jam. A few board games and a deck of cards took up the rest of the space.

"He's supposed to be going home tomorrow," she said.

Max shrugged. "It doesn't hurt to be prepared."

"Can I have a few crackers?" Brandon asked.

Half an hour later, they were snacking and playing a very competitive game of War with the cards when Max's cell phone rang.

"Seth, this better be important," he said as a greeting.

Camille didn't eavesdrop deliberately, but Max did nothing to keep her from hearing his end of the conversation.

"Seriously? That didn't take long," he said after a minute.

"I suppose she should know," was his next remark, followed by a glance her way.

"I'm going to be tied up until at least some time tomorrow. If the deal falls through, it falls through," he said eventually before ending the call.

"I don't want all of this to get in the way of some important deal," Camille said as he put the phone away.

"You're just trying to distract me so that you can beat me at cards," he countered. "But I have all the aces now. You'll never win."

They played until Brandon started falling asleep with his cards in his hand.

"Rest now," Camille said, hoping that the crackers he'd eaten while playing would actually stay in his stomach. "I'll be here all night."

"You have to wake me every hour," he reminded her sleepily.

"I will," she promised.

"One of us will, anyway," Max said. "If we take turns, we might both get some sleep."

Brandon nodded and then shut his eyes. Camille moved away from the bed, switching off lights as she went. Max cleared away the cards and the snacks and then sat down on the couch in the corner of the room. When Camille looked over at him, he patted the space next to him.

"Why are you here?" she demanded as she perched on the edge of the couch.

"Sit back and relax," he suggested. "Your head still hurts, doesn't it?"

"A bit, but what about your deal? And what else are you supposed to be telling me?"

He sighed and then turned sideways, partly behind her.

Putting his hands on her shoulders, he began to massage her tensions away.

"Max, stop," she protested.

He immediately released her. "Sorry, I was trying to help."

"Why?"

"I told you before that I'd like to start over with you, to see where things might go if we try again. I never stopped loving you," he replied.

"If you love someone, you try to see them more than once every thirty years."

"When I left Ramsey, I convinced myself that what we'd had was nothing but a teenage romance. I was sure there were hundreds of other women out there for me. Maybe there are, but I've never found any of them. I kept myself busy, buried myself in my business and I told myself that I was happy. For the most part, I was happy, actually, right up until someone broke a headlight on my car and the only woman I've ever loved reappeared in my life. At that moment, I suddenly realized what I'd been missing for the past thirty years."

He was saying all the right things, but Camille forced herself to argue. "I don't trust you. I don't trust anyone anymore. You're responsible for Jason leaving again, if nothing else."

"I offered Jason a choice of three different jobs. One of the options was a job right here in Ramsey. He decided he wanted the job in the city and he decided that he wanted to start immediately. I told him that he could start any time in the next six months. He insisted on going back right away."

"Was the job in New York a better one?"

"All three jobs were essentially the same, only in different locations," he told her.

"So he could have stayed here, if he'd wanted to," she sighed. "I shouldn't be surprised, really."

"He quit this afternoon."

"He quit this afternoon," she repeated slowly.

"That was one of the reasons why Seth called. He wanted me to know and he thought you might want to know, too."

"Did he give Seth a reason why he was quitting?"

"He told Seth that he'd decided he wasn't ready to go back to working again yet. He wants more time to be a free spirit, unbounded by the shackles of modern society."

Camille took a deep breath and then slowly counted to ten. "I hate him," she whispered when she'd reached ten.

"I don't blame you. He's an idiot. I thought maybe he'd come back when he heard about Brandon. What did he say when you called him?"

"Not much. He was glad that Brandon is okay, but he was with a woman and couldn't really talk."

Max sighed. "I'm sorry. There's a very selfish part of me that's glad he's out of your life, though. This would be a lot harder if you and he were still married."

"He's made it impossible for me to trust anyone."

"I'm not asking you trust me. I'm asking you to agree to try to learn to trust me," he countered. "Just give me a chance."

She shut her eyes. Her head was pounding and she couldn't think straight.

"Let me rub your shoulders," he whispered. "I promise it will help."

A tiny nod of her head was all the encouragement he needed. As he rubbed, she could feel some of the day's tension lifting. After several minutes, she began to relax.

"You need some sleep," he said in her ear.

"You should go home."

"The chair is a recliner. You sleep there and I'll sleep on the couch."

She looked at the small couch and shook her head. "You won't fit on the couch."

"I'll manage."

"You don't have to stay."

"I know I don't have to stay, but I want to stay. I want to be here for you. You've been doing all of this by yourself for years. You should be grateful to have some help."

"What happens when you get bored with Ramsey again?"

"I never got bored with Ramsey, I just wanted to see the rest of the world. I've seen it now and I can promise you there isn't anywhere else out there quite like our little home town. I said before that I hadn't realized that I'd been missing out on anything until I saw you again, but that isn't completely true. Driving back into Ramsey for the first time in thirty years made me realize that I'd been missing home for all of those years. Being in Ramsey makes me happier than I ever thought it could. I meant what I said at the fair. I'm going to be doing a lot for the town and for the good people who call it home."

"You've only been back a few weeks and you already left again once."

"I'm not going to promise that I'm never going to leave. I still want to travel sometimes, and I have business interests all over the world, but Ramsey is going to be home from now on. I made an offer on the Alexander mansion this morning. It may cost me a fortune, but I'm going to restore it to its former glory and make it my home."

"Really?" Camille gasped. "I can't wait to see what you do with it."

He chuckled. "At least that suggests that you're willing to see me again, even if it is just so you can see the mansion."

"I'm tired and my head aches and I don't know what I'm saying," she said quickly.

He stopped massaging and gently turned her to face him.

"Just give me a chance," he said softly. "I'll spend the rest of my life proving to you that I'm not dumb enough to let you get away again."

The kiss was gentle and full of promise and repressed passion. The night was uncomfortable. The recliner was lumpy and the couch was too short, but they did their best to rest in between the hourly alarms where they took turns waking Brandon and making sure he was okay. By morning, Camille was starting to believe that Max truly did care for her. Which was good, because she already knew she was crazy in love with him.

Second Act
A Later in Life Love Story
Release Date: June 19, 2020

Terri Briggs is happily divorced. She and her ex-husband get along reasonably well as they work together to raise their son, Thomas.

Lucas Hogan owns businesses all over the world, including several in Ramsey. He's never visited the small town, though.

When Lucas does pay a surprise visit to Ramsey, he has a shocking proposition for Terri. His dying mother wants to see him happily married before she dies, and he's prepared to pay Terri for her time if she'll pretend to be his fiancée for a few weeks.

Although Terri hates the idea of living a lie, Lucas insists that it's just a bit of harmless play-acting for a good cause. She reluctantly agrees and the Ramsey Harvest Festival gives them plenty of opportunities to be together. When Terri finds herself falling for Lucas, though, she starts to regret her decision.

ACKNOWLEDGMENTS

Thank you to my editor, Dan, for his hard work.

Thank you to Linda, who did the incredibly beautiful cover for this book.

And thank you readers, for giving this book a try. I hope you enjoyed reading it as much as I enjoyed writing it!

ABOUT THE AUTHOR

Diana Xarissa lived on the Isle of Man for more than ten years before returning to the United States with her family. Now living near Buffalo, New York, she enjoys having the opportunity to write about the island that she loves so much. It truly is a special place.

Diana also writes mystery/thrillers set in the not-too-distant future under the pen name "Diana X. Dunn" and fantasy/adventure books for middle grade readers under the pen name "D.X. Dunn."

She would be delighted to know what you think of her work and can be contacted through snail mail at:

Diana Xarissa Dunn

PO Box 72

Clarence, NY 14031.

You can sign up for her monthly newsletter on the website and be among the first to know about new releases, as well as find out about contests and giveaways and see the answers to the questions she gets asked the most.

Find Diana at:
www.dianaxarissa.com
diana@dianaxarissa.com

Made in United States
Orlando, FL
21 June 2023

34389858R00107